THE
HAWKS
OF
CHELNEY

By Adrienne Jones

THUNDERBIRD PASS

WHERE EAGLES FLY

RIDE THE FAR WIND

WILD VOYAGEUR

SAIL, CALYPSO!

ANOTHER PLACE, ANOTHER SPRING

THE MURAL MASTER

SO, NOTHING IS FOREVER

THE
HAWKS
OF
CHELNEY

Adrienne Jones

DRAWINGS BY
STEPHEN GAMMELL

Harper & Row, Publishers
New York, Hagerstown,
San Francisco, London

Library of Congress Cataloging in Publication Data
Jones, Adrienne.
    The hawks of Chelney.

    SUMMARY: The superstitious people of an isolated coastal village
ostracize a young boy because of his love for the wild ospreys they
believe are evil.
    I. Gammell, Stephen. II. Title.
PZ7.J677Haw   [Fic]   77-11855
ISBN 0-06-023057-6
ISBN 0-06-023058-4 lib. bdg.

For my grandson and granddaughter,
Jason C. Carter and Jaimi Camille Carter,
who have already enlivened the world by
their presence in it. May they add to
its loves and joys, and soften its hates
and sorrows in their lifetime.

Contents

THE
HAWKS
OF
CHELNEY

PART ONE

The Outcast

1

The village of Chelney stood beside the sea. To the north lay wide marshlands and estuaries and sand flats. Offshore were countless small islands, their fringes littered with driftwood. On rare occasions the driftwood was laced with decaying debris from some unlucky vessel driven on the hidden reefs by sudden gales and wicked currents. None of these islands were large enough to support a settlement, though from time to time one might provide shelter for some solitary fisherman caught out by an unexpected squall. And on the lee shores numerous seals basked and frolicked and mated during their season.

To the south of Chelney there were no shoals or islands, only the open sea, and along the sea's landward rim rose a jut of cliff streaked white from eons of bird droppings. Beneath the droppings the stone was dark and forbidding. In places it thrust to a great height and was scarred with ledges and shallow caves that offered nesting places for a few eagles and a myriad of lesser birds.

This year a male osprey had come early in the spring, an unusual occurrence, for no ospreys had been sighted here for almost a decade. A mate had joined him late in April. The waters along this particular stretch plunged to a great depth a few yards offshore. Thus they failed to provide a sufficient supply of the shallow-swimming fish these two elegant sea hawks required. Still, the pair seemed willing to make the longer flight to the estuaries for food. They had built a great nest halfway up the cliff on a flat shelf. The low spine of rock that stood at the edge would guard the nestlings from the danger of a fall to the harsh shore. On the shelf the ospreys found the remains of an old nest, a relic from years before. They added to this base, thrusting in sticks and husks and seaweed and all manner of rough material until the whole seemed an immense heap of flotsam cast up by some impossible wave.

The village clung to the windswept curve of land between estuaries and cliff. The shallow harbor there at Chelney offered anchorage for the small fishing boats that provided the people's livelihood. Since their fate hung upon the whims of nature, the villagers had drawn together in a tight protective community. They clung to the old ways and seemed of another century, frowning on any frivolity they felt might endanger them all. Even the children, blond and sturdy, tended to soberness. At one time, authorities outside and far away from Chelney had sent a schoolmaster to teach the children the newest knowledge to fit them for life in the world as it had become. The parents tolerated him for two seasons, then sent him away and returned to teaching the children in their own fashion. Except for infrequent visits of the *Sea Horse*, a little supply vessel meant to sustain isolated coastal villages, the authorities forgot about Chelney.

South of the village in a cottage set apart from the others lived an old man and his wife, Giles and Emma Duquesne. They had a son, Siri, born to them when the wife was past the usual age of childbearing. In the beginning, the villagers thought the boy a blessing at last bestowed on the barren old pair. But the boy grew up wild. He was unlike the other children of Chelney. After a time the people decided that instead of a blessing, Siri was a curse visited upon the couple for some hidden evil of theirs. But the Old Man and the Old Woman, weary with hard work and many trying years, left the boy to grow in any way he would.

In any event, by his fourteenth year and at the edge of manhood, Siri was shunned by the villagers. The Old Man treated him scarcely better. Siri seemed an alien spirit. He hated the cramped life of the fishing boats and the dour nature of the men. His long thin legs weren't meant for squatting over the endless tasks of unsnarling lines or gutting fish or mending nets. Whenever he could, he slipped away to run in the wild places beyond the village. There he would throw his voice across the windswept marshes, or send it racketing up among the crannies and the great faces and chimneys of the cliffs. But when he was with the Old Man he had to stay silent and submissive in deference to the other fishermen. Even then, the boy's large hands and feet were forever fumbling or stumbling or creating some nuisance that made the Old Man snort with anger.

Now the two seldom spoke with each other, and one day when another boy from the village showed himself eager to sail with the Old Man,

Siri was free to go his own way entirely. After that even the Old Woman began to withdraw her own cool affection; this was not her good child of earlier years. She remembered it was during his seventh summer that the boy had begun to explore the fingers of land that probed the estuaries and tideflats. Then the Old Woman had still been loath to let him go. The Old Man was little company and the baby had brightened her days. But slowly, it seemed to her, the boy had drawn away and changed. Now she scarcely knew him. She resented that Siri seemed forever hungry, and that he turned to her and home only when his belly was empty. So at dawn each day she swept him out of the house, and she began to guard the larder with the greedy vulgarity of the gulls that scrabbled over the village garbage. Yet from time to time she looked at him with sad and longing eyes; she had hoped for a child who would comfort her old age. Siri's black fierce gaze would stab back at her until she sighed and turned away and took up her bitter ways again.

So at fourteen, Siri found little to hold him to village or home. Only at nighttime would he return. Before dawn he was up and gone again. When the flocks came winging down from the north in September or sweeping up from the south in April, as now, a strange wild delight seized him. Then he raced over the miles of low ridges or along the beaches, arms stretched wide, flinging his voice at the calling flocks. With his dark hair abristle above broad forehead and straight ridge of brow, and his slender bony face lit by fierce eyes and ruled by a prominent nose, Siri seemed a bird himself. Spindly-limbed, large of foot and hand, light-boned but with a strong airy grace, he was a creature of the tidelands.

This Siri was unknown to the people of Chelney, for they perceived him as clumsy of mind and body, cursed of spirit. He was the wicked joy that struggled to arise in their own hearts with each coming of spring. When the Old Man forced him to work with the fishermen, they glowered and grumbled over his impossible behavior. Had the boy not collapsed with laughter the day Bartel Sunderman's boat broke its mooring and went scudding out to sea before the wind as surely as though piloted by Sunderman himself? Half a day of good labor was wasted in its recapture. And there was the time a line had snapped, loosing a net that bulged with the morning's catch. The snared hoard had flashed away, disappearing in the depths like spinning silver coins. Thus the labor of that morning also had been for naught, and the fishermen did not forget that Siri had shouted with outrageous glee to see that finny dash for freedom. Increasingly they ignored the impossible boy.

The children were told to shun him, but the older boys chased after him with threats or taunts when he passed through Chelney. Occasionally they cornered him. Then they would form a circle about Siri and take pleasure in detailing the things they planned for him if he did not stay clear of Chelney. But even when they twisted his arms, he would not cry to please them.

Once, their boyish laughter high and tense over what they intended to do, they dragged him to the shore and dug a pit at the water's edge. A pirates' trick from long ago. Siri fought so fiercely it required four of them to hold him in the pit while the others filled it in with sand to his chin. It took some time for the tide to rise. He was silent throughout the ordeal until the first reaching wave engulfed his head for an eternity. After that they dug him out, let him go. Siri hated the memory of his one strangled scream when the water had receded. In nightmares the terror returned; once more the packed sand held all his body, his arms, his fingers, his legs, his toes as still as death, while his eyes at ground level watched the capricious waves advance and recede and advance again. And then that taste of true death beneath the first wave.

He continued to go through Chelney. His pride required this of him. But wary now, more fleet of foot than the others, familiar with the hidden paths beyond the village, he easily eluded his harriers and left them behind.

During his early years along the shore, Siri had learned to catch the shallow-water fish. Now, in this year when he seemed truly outcast, he used this skill to feed himself. He took only enough to satisfy his needs. The snared fish, scaled and cleaned, sliced thinly, eaten fresh and raw with only a little salt he had taken from the Old Woman's kitchen or with a bit of wild onion, kept him through the bright windy days. He became as lean and bony and long-legged as the stilt sandpiper. And as enduring.

He haunted the wild-made paths and devious ways of his shimmering world. The seabirds and small rodents became his only companions. Mice and rabbits scurried among the bunchy sand grasses. Sleek otters and fat muskrats swam the winding waterways. In the marshes back from the sea, where the inland streams kept the water clear of salt, stood the gaunt and voracious cranes. Busy little rails and gallinules, able and quick when afoot, scuttled through the reeds and grasses; yet awkward in flight, they dropped wearily to ground after any aerial effort. The coots set

Siri off in his free laughter. At his sudden appearance they would half arise from the hidden ponds. Their strange scalloped feet pattered the water's surface as they skittered this way and that. But unless forced by some terror greater than the silent boy, they refused to take wing and at last collapsed into the pond again, scolding him with raucous cries.

"Fearful and stubborn as the people of Chelney." Siri laughed aloud. "The world is a serious place to them." And the coots, their dark rumps and white-tipped tails identical, would disappear all together among the reeds and rushes.

But Siri preferred the open sand flats and the shore to the secret marshes. Here the wind blew sweet and clean, and the sound of the sea filled him. Even the birds seemed more companionable. The phalaropes, the stilts, the avocets; the snipes and sandpipers and willets; the sanderlings in little flocks, like clockwork miniatures on twinkling feet. And of course the gulls—the gregarious, screaming, restless gulls, winging and wheeling or gliding the everlasting air currents, or squabbling among themselves over any scrap of food. Of all these, it was the sandpipers he loved. They ran constantly before his feet, flashed up and over and behind him, and kept him company on his solitary way.

Sometimes, when he became too desperately lonely, he would fasten his mind on the schoolmaster who had come to Chelney and stayed for two seasons. How alike they were in their solitude, for the people had scorned the man and his knowledge; and the children, urged by their parents, had closed their minds against him. But those days remained in Siri's thoughts—how he and the schoolmaster had become friends, had roamed the wild land about Chelney and talked together, each learning from the other. The man instructed Siri in the scientific knowledge of the wild things, told him their names, explained the marvelous structures of skeleton and musculature, the way each species fitted into the intricate whole so one sustained the other. And in turn the man glimpsed new views through the boy's acute, observing eyes while Siri led him along the secret estuary ways. Though the man was sent from Chelney after those two seasons, Siri had not forgotten that shining time. And now it came back to console him.

During the second week of June, Siri saw the osprey for the first time. He could scarcely believe his good fortune, for no osprey had been sighted along the Chelney coast in recent years. The fish hawk was hunting at the mouth of the largest estuary, nearly half a mile offshore. The day was bright and the bird flew well above the water's surface, perhaps to keep its shadow from the prey it sought. The hawk's dive caught Siri's eye.

Nearly three hundred feet aloft, the bird set its wings and plunged into the water talons first. It disappeared beneath the surface, but presently struggled up, labored mightily with its wings in a rapid horizontal motion, rose straight into the air, then with a powerful sweep was off and away. A fish struggled in its talons. The captured prey was nearly as long as the osprey's body and glinted in the sun as it twisted to free itself from the great hooks that held it fore and aft.

At first, Siri had thought the bird a bald eagle, for the head seemed white and the wingspread was almost six feet. But as it tilted overhead, Siri saw that its crown was dark-streaked and a narrow mask of blackish feathers extended from beak to eyes to nape. The whole of the bird's underparts was white except for dusky banding on the spread tail and a scattering of brown spots on the breast. As the osprey banked steeply in a turn, Siri noted that the back and upper surface of the wing and tail were mahogany in color, of a shade so rich that it cast a purple iridescence in the sunlight.

Despite the burning energy of his body, the boy

remained motionless on the sandbar as the osprey circled the wide sky and wheeled off to the south, carrying its catch headfirst into the wind. The bird did not alight to satisfy its own hunger.

"A mate somewhere, hungry on her nest," Siri said softly.

He knew he was right when, after a bit, the hawk returned, its talons empty, to continue the hunt. This time, unsuccessful at the estuary mouth, the bird widened its circle of flight. Siri, as still as beached driftwood, felt the racing of his own heart. The osprey stirred some unknown thing within him. Fear flared for a moment, but was gone the next as a rabbit lopped past scarcely an arm's length away. Unhungry and aimless in this summertime world of plenty, it did not see the boy.

Suddenly the little puff-tailed buck was seized by a premonition of danger. Wing shadows darkened his view for a flick of time. He dashed for cover. That first lazy amble had caught the osprey's sharp roving gaze. Now at the rabbit's frenzied motion, the hawk swept low over the bar. So swiftly did it come that its swoop crossed the path of the frantic leaper. The bird was gone, returned to its fishing, before the rabbit found his burrow. Siri laughed. He knew that the fish hawk

15

had little taste for warm blood. It seemed to have been playing a game to break the tension of its serious work.

The laugh lingered in Siri's eyes. "If only the people of Chelney could do the same," he whispered.

But his thoughts dodged quickly to other things. How many eggs did the ospreys have in that nest off to the south? When would they hatch? How long before the female could leave the fledglings and join her mate in the hunt? For eventually it would take the efforts of both to satisfy the growing appetites of their young. Siri's mind sailed the air currents with the solitary osprey who spiraled there against the high blue. In fancy the boy crested the wind tides himself, rose up and up above the estuaries, curved over Chelney in one great circle, then slanted south in a long glide. He dreamed that he thrust in where the updrafts climbed the forbidding cliffs, then tilted to land with precision on a narrow ledge. Above him the rampart of rock sliced the wind-swept sky. Below, the breakers foamed at its foot. The sea stretched far off to the horizon. From this height the restless water, patterned like overlaid fish scales, glittered in the spring light.

The daydream had brought an uneasy vertigo, but now, on the sandbar, Siri sprang to his feet.

For a moment he watched the osprey, who had gone back to the mouth of the estuary. Again Siri felt that sharp quickening of fear. His eyes darkened and his stomach shrank painfully within him. He gave a fierce cry, snatched back the part of him that had flown with the sea hawk. The boy's great feet thrust at the sand, he leaped away, running over the spit of land. At the end of the estuary he splashed headlong through the shallow waters, and turned toward Chelney. He fled from the wild loneliness of the empty tidelands.

It was dusk when Siri loped through Chelney. Strangely, tonight, the sight of the cottages comforted him. They were all lit from within; the lamps cast an orange glow through the light scrim curtains or heavier ones of yellowed lace. Families gathered about dinner tables, or sat relaxed and sated before fires built to give cheer rather than winter warmth, for the evening was not cold. The good smell of cooking food was on the air.

"Will the Old Woman have something for me?" Siri asked the night. When he was little, he had called her Emma. And the Old Man Giles. Perhaps even then they had seemed too ancient, too distant in time to call them Mother, Father. Now he followed the way of the villagers and thought of them only as the Old Woman and the Old Man.

By the time Siri had reached the house beyond the village, he had forgotten the fear inspired by the osprey. Inside, he saw that the Old Man and the Old Woman nodded in their chairs. Scraps of dinner still lay on the plates in the untidy kitchen. The couple must have been very tired tonight. Usually the Old Woman was more than neat in everything she did.

Siri swallowed the leavings, filched half a loaf of bread and a nub of cheese from the cupboard. He would eat some beneath the blankets and save the rest for tomorrow. Without waking the couple, he went to bed.

That night he dreamed he flew with the ospreys. They seemed unafraid of the terrible sea of air and the awful space, empty and murmurous, below them. Siri awoke before dawn and found that a fog had crept in from the sea during the night. But he was sweating despite the chill of the damp air.

2

June edged toward July. The days were filled
with sun and fair winds, enabling the village fleet
to stay out from dark to dark. The fish had appeared in massed silvery hordes this year. The
villagers lamented that their boats were small and
ill-equipped for long voyages such as those made
by downcoast fishermen. Still, they did what they
could and each prospered. The men became arro-
gant and proud; they ascribed this good fortune to
some great skill on their part.

But a few did recall the lean years and knew
that in reality Chelney's fate hung on the fine

thread of chance. Who could tell where the fish would run each spring and summer? So these few began to mull over the old superstitions and to wonder what magic had brought them such a favorable season. And darkly, fearfully, they began to ask the others, what curse might break the spell and turn good fortune to bad? The questions spread and ran like a dark current below the surface of arrogance and pride.

This was the first season that Siri was not included in the work of the hard-pressed men. Even the Old Woman asked nothing of him. It was as though he had ceased to exist.

Siri laughed and said to himself, "If I had died they would have mourned me."

At first this made little difference to him. Instead he was glad to follow his own ways. But each evening he went through the village to reach home, for he still slept there. As the days passed, the sight of the people inside their houses began to make him lonely. He would remember how the Old Woman had touched him gently when he was small, the tender looks that had passed from her to him and back again. Then for a moment he would wonder that such a chill distance had grown between them. The pain of his loneliness would force him to a faster trot that carried him quickly past the houses, as closed against him as the Old Woman's heart.

Yet during the long daylight hours, he forgot he was an outcast; his whole being had become absorbed in a continuing watch of the osprey. The bird hunted all the estuaries and the shallow waters offshore, but never the same place two days in succession. Each dawn, Siri arrived at the previous day's hunting grounds. There the luminous sky held only the wheeling gulls and smaller seabirds. Scanning the horizon, Siri would discover the osprey—small in the distance, yet unmistakable with its sudden plummeting dive and its great wings bent oddly at the alula.

Then Siri would race across the narrow sandy fingers to settle directly beneath where it circled. Several times he thought it took notice of him, sweeping in to look him over with fierce golden eyes. Then it tilted up and off again to the hunt.

By the end of June, Siri had discerned a pattern to its daily moves. In a cycle of five days, the bird shifted from the most southerly portion of the estuaries to the most northerly, first seaward then inland in a general zigzag progression. On each sixth day it returned to the first site and the cycle began again. Though this knowledge saved him some effort, Siri still covered great distances. His sinewy legs grew thinner, but were tireless racing over the miles. The ribs and muscles of his chest expanded so he was never winded. But in actuality he worked harder than any man of Chelney.

The osprey obsessed his mind. In fancy he was almost osprey himself. When the hawk slanted across the land, Siri ran swiftly in its shadow, arms wide, tilting, whirling, turning. When the great bird sailed out across the sea or the wide estuaries, Siri remained poised at the edge of the water as though he also would launch himself up and up into the high blue. Each time the hawk gave its harsh scream, Siri's thin voice came in echo. At first these human sounds startled the osprey and it would wheel up and away, diminishing against the sky. Then the boy would cry in despair and frustration.

But as the days passed, Siri's ear became atuned to the variations of pitch, the cadence of the hawk's calls. His voice expanded and changed. Early one morning, on that day's first sighting of the hawk, Siri flung a great harsh cry into the brightening sky. This time, miraculously, the hawk turned on a wing tip, plummeted down. It swept so close that the bird's primaries brushed the boy's face. For a fraction of time the round golden gaze had stared directly into Siri's eyes. He leaped and called and laughed and called again, delirious with joy as the hawk answered and sailed in time after time.

Yet despite this friendship between osprey and boy, occasionally the strange fear returned and shook Siri as it had that first day. He would sink down, shivering, a flightless silent creature crouched there upon the open sand. Then loneliness crushed him. Finally he would spring up and run back toward the village. There he roamed the outskirts, and from a distance hungrily watched the children at their stolid play. But one day he found if he endured the fear, ignored the loneliness, and remained among the estuaries, he became used to those emotions and the desolation faded. Waking or sleeping, in dreams he sailed with the ospreys, one of their winged tribe, no longer Siri, the outcast of Chelney.

At the beginning of July, two things happened that changed the tenor of Siri's days. The first was the result of his own resolve; the second had to do with a certain plan devised by the men of Chelney. The resolve arose from a sudden urge to find the nest that hung upon the face of the guano-streaked cliffs south of the village. Thus, one morning before dawn, instead of going to the estuaries, Siri took the opposite direction and climbed the steep slope of land that led to the cliffs.

There below was Chelney. The early lights of the fishing boats went bobbing out to sea for the day's work. The lamps in the houses made a small constellation in the dark. He could even distinguish the cottage that belonged to the Old Man and Old Woman, set apart as it was from the others. Again he remembered dimly that the Old Woman had loved him there when he was small. They had laughed together, and she had fondled him, running a finger over the childish down that grew along his spine and hazed the flat of his back above the round buttocks. "My little dove," she had breathed in her rough whisper. But that was long ago.

Now before him lay an unknown land. He had never explored here. It was a forbidding place, full of wind and the threat of storm even when the sun shone elsewhere. He hesitated, glanced once more at Chelney, then pushed on. The way along the shore would have been more direct, but the tide was running and the waves crashed against the precipice with brutal force. A rise of hill cut into the cliffs above the reach of the water. Siri found a safe cranny there and settled to his task.

The early watch went unrewarded. He remembered the osprey was always above the estuaries at dawn. Thus it must have left the nest before the sky brightened and so he had failed to see it. Still, the hawk would return to its ledge by sunset. Or surely he would see it when it brought fish to its mate and young perched hungrily somewhere above.

Siri waited through the day. He saw an eagle or two but no osprey. He had not reckoned on the vastness of the cliffs. When night fell he gave up the vigil and returned to Chelney. During the past weeks he had seldom seen the Old Man and the Old Woman. Yet some spark of affection must have remained hidden in the woman's heart, for there was always a bit of food left to hand each night when Siri crept through the kitchen past the room of the sleeping pair. This night was no exception. But instead of the usual fish, there was a bit of meat, some fresh berries, and also a spoonful or two of honey for the coarse bread. He wondered if she had deprived herself to leave such delicacies for him. The thought of this made his chest hurt and he blinked to clear his vision. Nevertheless, he quickly consumed the food for he was very hungry.

The next morning he returned to the cliffs, but again failed to see the osprey. Nor did the third day bring success. It was at the end of this third day that the fear and unrest of the whole village came to his attention, and also the plan devised by the Chelney men to end their misfortune. After nightfall, when Siri came trotting down the slope from the cliffs, he saw that most of the village was dark. The only exception was the Meeting House. Tonight it stood a beacon. Obviously something of importance was afoot, and the Chelney Council had been called to session.

This Council was composed of the active fishermen of the village, though even the women attended from time to time to voice opinions. Still, it was the men who made the decisions. The Leader of the Council was chosen by lot. This year it had fallen to Bartel Sunderman, a man not much respected by the others, for he was a bully. Nevertheless he was now Leader.

Tonight, even from the hillside, Siri could see people passing in through the big double door of the Meeting House. Men, women, and children. He knew his eyes had sharpened during this season, but the clarity of detail he could perceive surprised him now. There were the Old Man and the Old Woman entering with the others. And Bartel Sunderman, who swaggered a little, full of his own importance.

Siri was bone tired, but curiosity carried him past his own cottage and on into Chelney. It was warm this first week of July and the windows and doors of the Meeting House were open. The murmur of voices flowed out through the night, a small river of sound, dissonant and babbling. He reached the building and concealed himself below a window. There was no need to see what was going on; one meeting was much like another. Presently Sunderman struck the table with a heavy fist to silence them all, and the meeting began.

After a few minutes Siri yawned. What a fool he had been to come! Sunderman was making the usual announcements of village events—marriages, deaths, births, successes, failures, evildoings of a few of the inhabitants. Siri smiled. Evil? Who dared do evil in this village! A little secret tippling, a man who struck his wife too hard or too often, a woman who flirted more openly than the others with the handsome fellow who kept the village store, a man who touched a curve of someone's unwilling daughter.

Yet why, Siri wondered, was every Chelnian here tonight? Usually half the village found excuses to stay at home. Exhausted from the long day, he dozed. It was Sunderman's voice, loud, full of bluster, that reached out and disturbed him. The words entered Siri's mind and brought him sharply awake.

"—some curse fallen upon us. That is the only answer. Who reads the signs? Can none among you—"

A woman interrupted. "The only curse in Chelney is timidity! If you would sail farther out to sea, you'd find the fish again! You've forgotten you are men!"

Sunderman growled at her audacity, but the woman persisted. "Surely the ocean isn't empty of fish!" Her voice leaped angrily from the window above Siri's head. Sunderman banged the table to silence her.

But another woman joined in. "We ask you, Bartel Sunderman, how can the best season in memory turn sour overnight?"

Then a third. "Empty nets for nearly two weeks! If things don't get better, we'll be forced to begin on the fish salted for the winter."

Now Sunderman's heavy voice overrode them. "Eric Ganney's boat went too far last Friday," he shouted. "Have you forgotten he did not return?"

Ganney's wife began to cry. The child in her lap whimpered. Despite this, Sunderman's words turned brutal. "There's no hope for them. Ganney was an able sailorman. He'd have brought back crew and vessel by now if still afloat."

All the people fell silent, except the child who continued to cry. It was the Old Man who finally spoke. He was the eldest active fisherman of Chelney and daily captained his own craft, so all listened to him with respect.

"The season started well in April. We were proud and said to ourselves, 'The village prospers because we are such fine fishermen.' Now we see it was only luck brought the fish our way. It had nothing to do with skill. But what changed our good luck to bad? Can you answer that?" He looked around wisely as though he had half solved the problem with his question.

The people stared at one another and shrugged. Again silence settled in the room. Sunderman stood glowering at the people. It was the Old Woman who broke the spell.

"If evil spirits have blighted our fortune, surely there's some way to drive them out." She fixed Sunderman with a baleful gaze. Life had treated her meanly, so now it gave her pleasure to badger the man. "Eh, Bartel Sunderman, what say you? You were rooster proud when the Leader's lot fell to you. Now you call us to meeting and fill the night with questions. Have you no answers to solve our difficulties?"

Siri could hear a sigh sweep the room. He rose and peered in the window. None noticed him, for all eyes were on the Old Woman. Cleverly she let the silence do its work, and presently the people began to look from one to another. Then, slowly, all turned to fix Sunderman with hostile gazes. A cloud of anger gathered in the room, and at any moment the fear at its center would strike some exposed and handy target. There Sunderman stood. Even a dull man turns clever to save his own skin.

He spoke quickly. "Of course the cause of our trouble is clear to me. As Leader I watch all that goes on within the village. And further, Old Woman, I have been seeking some sign from sky or land or sea that would tell me what has blighted our fishing. Now I know for a certainty what evil it is that has stolen our good fortune."

"Then give us the answer and let us deal with this evil that you claim to have found," she cried.

"I only wanted all to have a fair chance to voice an opinion before I spoke."

"Eh, noble of you! We'll voice our opinion *after* you have your say."

Laughter went round the room. It was an unpleasant sound. Sunderman coughed a little; his eyes watered. When he spoke, the words came slowly. The people's anger swelled as they listened to his aimless talk.

"To a thinking man," he began, "it is quite clear what has driven the fish from the waters of Chelney. Let me explain. It would all be quite simple if there had been storms during the past weeks. Storms would have driven the fish too deep for our nets, then we would know why our holds are empty. But there have been no storms."

He paused. A disconcerting mutter rose among the listeners. He took a quick breath and rushed on. "The sea currents hereabout are as usual, neither too hot nor too cold. An extreme either way might have caused the fish to seek a more pleasant spot. And we have worked as hard and with the same skill as when our hatches were filled each day. So it is neither laziness nor poor methods that are to blame."

A fresh gust of impatience swept the room. Sunderman's little eyes, set wide apart in his flat face, darted here and there seeking some escape from his predicament. There seemed to be none, so he blundered ahead.

"We have not stinted on the time spent at fishing. Each man has sailed before dawn and returns near dark. I myself come into harbor after the chickens have gone to roost. My smaller children clamor for dinner. They have eaten and are abed by the time I come ashore. My older ones are in from their chores and at table and served when I open the door. Even—" And here Sunderman eased his own pain by digging at the Old Woman who had started all this. "—Even that odd one of yours, that Siri, comes slinking back through the dark from whatever he does out there in the wild tidelands. My own son Oren, who has followed him a time or two, says your Siri speaks only with the birds and animals. Everyone else avoids him."

At mention of his name, Siri shifted uneasily out there in the night. It was this movement that caught the desperate searching gaze of the miserable man. Sunderman paused in his rambling talk. As he stared at the boy, a look of calculation came into his eyes. Here was the answer. One that would solve his problem and perhaps make the Old Woman suffer for her temerity. Now he pointed toward the back of the room. Like many a dishonest man, Sunderman convinced himself on the instant that what he planned to do was right. After all, whatever the cost, a Leader must lead.

Every villager turned to stare at the boy framed there against the black night. At first they did not recognize him. If he could have seen himself, even Siri would have been startled at the change the wild weeks had made in him. His skin was brown and leather tough. The jutting nose and glittering eyes lent his thin face a predatory fierceness. His body had lengthened, but narrowed too, except for the high, fan-ribbed barrel of chest. The stringy whipcord arms, the steel grasp of his big hands on the window ledge drew an uneasy murmur from the villagers. They had almost forgotten there was a boy named Siri. Guilt whispered through the bottom of their minds and increased their anger. Sunderman pressed his advantage.

"There he stands! The root of all our troubles!"

The Old Woman's hand wandered to her mouth. She had thought as little as possible of Siri for the past weeks. It was enough that she left food for him on the kitchen table. What else could she do with so wild a boy? Now she did not understand the pain that stabbed her heart at the sight of him.

She covered her fright and said sourly, "You speak like a fool, Bartel Sunderman."

He ignored her and continued.

"We all know how Chelney's older boys find a little harmless sport in calling out at Siri. Sometimes they pursue him as he flies like a shadow through the village. Only in fun, of course. They're all good boys. My son Oren joins in the chase from time to time."

The villagers glanced at one another. It was Oren who led the harrying of Siri. Still, better that the burly brute take after that strange one than bully their own sons. Besides, what harm in hounding the solitary boy? No one had ever really hurt him. So they all nodded. Sunderman thought they were in agreement with him and continued.

"Oren is quick and strong, but he's not foolish enough to follow that one into the boggy tideflats. Nevertheless he has sometimes watched him from a distance." Sunderman's finger jabbed toward the window.

"It's no crime to wander those sand ridges or the shore," the Old Woman said. "It only needs sense enough to find the way and not be caught by changing tides."

But Sunderman had snared the interest of the others. Even the Old Man muttered, "Be quiet, wife." None noticed that Siri's gaze softened a little. The Old Woman had almost taken his part.

Sunderman went on. "Not more than two weeks ago when Oren drove Chelney's goats to the north pastures, he saw Siri sitting beside the nearest inlet at the edge of the flats. My boy paid him no mind until he noticed that a fish hawk hunted there. Several times it swooped low over Siri's head and, strangely, Oren heard the boy call out to it. The hawk answered."

"And what evil is there in a boy calling to birds?" the Old Woman said. At the window Siri smiled. He cared nothing for the others, yet it warmed him that at last the Old Woman was on his side.

But Sunderman leaned forward across the table

and fixed her with his little pike eyes. He spoke almost softly. "The evil lies in the fish hawk."

"Foolishness!" The Old Woman held her ground. "The evil lies in your mouth, Bartel. You only try to save yourself by weaving tales."

"It is handed-down lore that I learned from my grandmother who learned it from hers. The words of it are 'Where the sea hawk hunts, the fisherman hungers.'"

The Old Woman sniffed. "Fish hawks hunt close to shore, not out where you cast your nets."

But her words were lost in the talk that sprang from the others. They were eager for any solution.

Said one: "There are ancient myths of evil birds sent by Satan."

And a second: "The answer, then, is to kill the hawk."

Another: "There'd be no harm in that, and it might do some good."

A fourth: "At least it's worth a try."

Sunderman saw he was saved. Beyond that, while he had half convinced the villagers, he had fully convinced himself. The death of the hawk would bring good fortune back to Chelney. With his own hide secure, a brief generosity flickered to life. His voice turned hearty.

"Siri will do his part to help us. Everyone's skill

should count for something. Who knows the ways of the fish hawk better than Siri?"

"Aye," said the Old Man, pleased that his son was of some value at last. "He will help us with the hunt."

Hopefully the Old Woman turned toward Siri. Now they would see she had raised a proper son; his strange talent would save them all. But her pride was short-lived. The wild face at the window retreated. She reached toward where it hung for a moment in the square of lamplight. But he had vanished in the night.

Several men sprang up, leaped out through the doorway, and took off in close pursuit. Those in the Meeting House could hear the men's boots pounding off along the hard-packed Chelney road. The clatter receded, diminished, until finally there was only silence. Presently from out of the night came the distant echo of a harsh cry, as wild as a hawk's, piercing the black sky. But surely no bird could sound so anguished. The Old Woman began to weep silently.

After some time the men returned, empty-handed.

"It's as black as a cave out there," said one, "and we had no lantern. It was useless to search farther."

So they decided to wait until morning.

3

Siri had flown along the empty road. At first he heard shouts and the thud of feet behind him. He passed his own cottage without pause and fled on beyond into the countryside. There all was still. The sounds of pursuit had ceased entirely.

Free as the sea hawk, he told himself; what do I care for the people of Chelney! Yet his heart was not persuaded and when he tried to split the night sky with a shout of exultation, the terrible anguished cry that sprang from his throat had driven him back to silence. Now he only ran. Alone he leaped up the slopes below the cliff.

Finally he stumbled into a hollow beneath a tree. It was partially leaf filled, and sinking down there, he curled in upon himself. Neither sleep nor thought nor sensation of cold or damp came to him throughout the night. His only comfort was the dim knowledge that those in Chelney could never use him against the beautiful fierce hawk. What kind of boy would aid in the death of a friend?

The brightening sky surprised him, for he had had no sense of passing time. He arose before the sun and began to climb inland along a steep tortuous way that led toward the cliff top. By the time he stood at the edge of the high plateau where the sheer drop fell away to the rocky shore, the empty black mood of the night began to fade. As the fiery sun rolled above the horizon, his heart lifted.

He gave no further thought to the village. He fastened his mind on the search for the hawks as he began to make his way along the lip of the plateau. From time to time he lay prone, thrusting his head and shoulders over the windy void to study the crags below. All up and down the cliffs seabirds roosted singly, in pairs, or in noisy clusters. Even now flocks tilted off into the breezy air to start this day's urgent search for food.

Scattered among the countless cracks and crannies were a number of ledges. On two of these at widely separated points he discovered the piled disorder of a hawk's nest. Each proved to be an eagle's aerie. Yet he was certain that somewhere here he would find the ospreys. Briefly he wondered if more than one pair was nesting on the cliffs this season, then decided it unlikely. The once-plentiful sea hawks had disappeared from Chelney's coast when he was still a child, perhaps driven off by the villagers, perhaps decimated by the poisons of civilization in their wintering grounds, or killed by hunters for the sport of it. Whatever the cause, the osprey he had seen over the estuaries was the only one to show itself here in recent years. Yet Siri had no doubt that a pair and young were somewhere below.

It occurred to him that the ledge he sought might be hidden from view beneath an overhang. The more he thought about this, the more likely it seemed. The ospreys would seek a sheltered ledge to hide their young from foraging eagles who would not discriminate between warm blood and cold. Scaled or furred or feathered, any prey was welcome to them.

When noontime hunger seized him, he wondered what he could find to quiet it. Among the estuaries and marshes food presented little difficulty. But on this plateau only wind-stunted pines, sparse grass, and a few gnarled, woody shrubs managed to exist in the scant soil that overlaid the rock core. As his hunger increased, Siri thought of the possibility of eggs. There might be a few, laid fresh by birds bereaved earlier in the season. Nests should be plentiful on the ledges below.

Siri found a chimney formation and began carefully to descend. His bony spine grated against one wall while hands and feet pressed firmly on the other. He used every hold and irregularity he could find and, undaunted by the windy empty space below, he worked his way down to an ample ledge. He was quite secure here, for the platform was at least thirty yards long and as wide as the Old Woman's kitchen. Birds flew off at his approach. Some ventured back or hovered nervously in midair as he inspected the nests, a great number of which, now in July, lay deserted. There were young birds, still unsteady in flight, and their watchful parents, but the empty nests gave ample evidence that many had hatched and grown and departed. There were no fresh eggs here, though he did find one nest, abandoned, with an unhatched egg, missed by the scavengers. The weathered shell assured it would be rotten and he passed it by. He looked for signs of eagle or osprey. There were none. At the end of the ledge he found a connecting shelf a few inches wide. It was precarious in some degree, but by now he was ravenous.

In his fancied flights with the ospreys, the open sea of air had terrified him. Now, in reality, he was unafraid. He edged along the narrow way, his cheek pressed lightly to the towering cliff, his hands delicately poised, palms against rock, for balance in the drafty breeze. At one point the shelf was broken, but three feet beyond at a slightly lower level it continued. With no hesitation, Siri straddled the gap. Between his long legs he glimpsed the thin lace edge of breakers a thousand feet below. His fingers curved, nails hooked into invisible holds. He pulled himself safely across. A light sweat beaded his upper lip, but he continued on with calm precision.

Presently there was another ledge, more expansive than that first below the chimney. Here among the empty nests he found two not yet deserted. Each of these was covered by a nervous kittiwake. Siri scared them up; they flew off to hover in the open space beyond the ledge, and screamed their treble-noted threats as he inspected the nests. The first held three eggs, buffy, freckled with brown and lavender. Carefully he removed one. There were four in the other nest, each smaller than a hen's egg, and after some hesitation he took two. On the far end of the ledge where it narrowed and sloped outward, he was surprised to see a single murre. Their great flocks usually gathered only on the offshore islands. Since no other birds were as gregarious as the sooty-backed, white-fronted murres, Siri wondered why this one was here alone. She crouched as though concealing her solitary egg with body and wings. He wished he could reassure the motionless creature. She would have laid the single egg on bare rock, and he'd not steal that and leave her destitute.

He cradled the kittiwake eggs carefully in his palm, and moved slowly toward the murre. The kittiwakes settled behind him, still crying plaintively. The murre remained motionless. On closer approach he saw she was dead. With one foot he lifted her toward the drop to the sea and tumbled her off. Murres were more birds of the water than the air, swimming so swiftly beneath the surface they could outdistance their finny prey. It satisfied Siri that the sea would take her now.

Where she had lain was the solitary egg, bulbous at one end, pointed at the other. When he rolled it with his foot, he marveled at how neatly it saved itself. The peculiar shape assured it would roll in a tight circle, never far enough to drop from the inhospitable bare ledge. He settled on this far end of the shelf out of sight of the kittiwakes. Rather than risk carrying the eggs, he broke them open one by one, swallowing the contents of each at a gulp.

He sat for a long while, staring over the flat sea. Off to the north he caught sight of the estuaries, and nearer, Chelney. To his surprise the boats were still at anchor in the harbor. Only out toward the horizon could he see any movement. There a coastwise steamer slid slowly down the sea's curve. Distance made it a toy ship. Siri tried to picture life on board—men working and sweating and laughing together, perhaps a half dozen passengers taking their ease on deck. At least he had heard this was the way of it, though he had little first-hand knowledge, since no craft of any significant size ever put in at Chelney. The islands and shoals and cliffs precluded this.

Any coastwise seaman in this quarter could chill the blood with tales of black storms that raged down from the arctic with no warning, and of the death of ships gale-driven upon the wicked Chelney reefs. Ships' captains gave the dangerous coast a wide berth even in fair weather. Only the supply vessel, the *Sea Horse*, made its infrequent runs to Chelney. Siri felt no envy of the people aboard the distant ship. He preferred it here—though his mind did linger a moment on the camaraderie of the men.

While he was musing, luck sailed in on the wind. A movement somewhere off to the left below caught his eye. A familiar slant of wings, a flash of rich mahogany, a striped crown above masked eyes. The osprey flew straight toward the cliff and disappeared from view. Beneath an overhang, as he had guessed. After a few minutes there was the osprey again; it dropped down into the slant of wind, rose on the updraft, and disappeared north against the projection of cliff. Siri waited. Presently another osprey appeared, larger than the first. This one flew in directly from the sea with a fish in her talons. So now both were a-wing. She, also, disappeared for a short time beneath the overhang, then was off once more to continue the constant hunt.

Siri was glad that hawks mature so slowly. He guessed there was a little time yet before the brood of young ospreys would take wing. As soon as they could fly, the old birds would abandon them to live or die by their own efforts. Instinct must provide the skill for the difficult feat of snatching fish from the sea. He knew that sometimes this skill did not come quickly enough, for he remembered the schoolmaster had said that

44

half the young ospreys did not survive their first season. Siri shuddered. Life had been hard for him, but no unlearned lesson had exacted that fatal punishment.

Urgency seized him to see beneath the lip that hid the ospreys' nest. But when he began to look for a way to edge across and down, it seemed that his good fortune was to fail him; beyond this present platform the scarp was smooth, devoid of ledges or cracks or chimneys or holds. Yet his gaze roved farther and came to rest on a faint green line that ran down an angle of the cliff and ended in a dark crevice near the overhang. Though his vision had sharpened beyond belief during these last weeks, the shadow of the angle made him uncertain. Was the vein green malachite or vegetation? He hoped it was grass or scrub; then footholds and handholds could be gouged. Perhaps.

Carefully he noted that the green line started beneath a stunted pine wedged there against the skyline. He sprang to his feet and returned along the ledge. Once again at its far end there was the narrow connecting shelf that must be traversed to reach the other safe and ample ledge. But this time the shelf's broken gap posed a new difficulty. Earlier, the slight difference in height of the two sections of shelf had been to his advantage for he had balanced across and down. Now the reverse would have to be accomplished; he must stretch to his fullest, then pull himself up to the higher level. Despite the danger, he straddled the airy space. Quickly, though, it became evident that he could not lift his weight to gain the higher side, for the handholds were at shoulder height and very small. He clutched at them so tightly his nails broke and his fingers bled.

The wind had become stronger. It snatched at him. For an instant he wavered. Should he retreat? But then he would be marooned. And no one would come to save him. His mind wheeled away as had the panicked kittiwakes. Slowly he coaxed it back, not looking at the empty space below or that flat creaming of waves on the rocky shore. He forced himself to study the nearby stone. At knee level he discovered a small projection, a miniature step for his left foot. This would halve the distance. He tested it. Yes, adequate. Yet once balanced there, he could not step with his right foot, for it was blocked by the left on that single perch. But, no longer stretched to the utmost, he stood higher than before and the reach of his arm was extended. Above he found an ample hold for one hand. In an instant he hoisted himself, exchanged feet on the step, and in a moment was safely across.

Now he shuddered in the afternoon breeze, for his clothes clung clammily to his bony body. He waited several minutes for the shaking in his arms and knees to subside. But he laughed at his triumph of the gap, and refused to think of the eventual hazard of the green vein that might lead him to the ospreys' ledge.

The ascent of the chimney was arduous. It took much longer than the morning's descent. By the time he reached the cliff's upper rim, the afternoon was waning. Further search would have to wait until morning. The heights were too cold for the night, so he made his way down once more to the base of the cliffs. It was dark by the time he reached the hillside below. The lights of Chelney, off there in the night, made him lonely. The Old Woman would be preparing dinner in the warmth of the kitchen. Would she forget and start to set a place for him? Restlessly he turned his back on Chelney's glow, fastened his mind on a search for some form of shelter. After a lengthy effort, he found a cave in the cliffs. By starlight, scavenging beneath the trees of the slope, he managed to find sufficient leaves and needles and springy branches to carry to his cave and build a makeshift nest.

He burrowed within the pungent rustling mass

for warmth and, despite his hunger, quickly fell asleep. The nights could be arctic-cold in winter, but July was a kind month. Exhausted from last night's stupor and his day on the ledges, Siri slept almost comfortably until early morning.

PART TWO

The Hunters

4

For the second day in a row no boats put out to sea from Chelney. Instead the men and older boys ate in the dark before dawn, donned boots if they owned a pair, took up whatever guns were available, and moved out into the countryside. Yesterday they had searched for that intolerable Siri; now they must begin the hunt for the osprey without him. They were certain that sooner or later he would return. Then they would force him to help in the destruction of the hawk.

On this morning they lined the shore of the first estuary, or concealed themselves in the reeds near the marshes. Now they waited. No breeze stirred. The fingers of water, pearled like the inner face of oyster shells, were ephemeral in the pale dawn. The sun breached the horizon. The air leaped to life, fractured the water's surface, and a myriad of flashing prisms dazzled the morning.

There was a rush of muted talk among the men and boys. Presently this died, as did the breeze. The day promised to be long and hot. There was no hint of mist or cloud to obscure the view across the flat expanse where countless sea and marsh birds skimmed the still air. The warm July silence was broken by their chatter and discordant cries. Gradually the tension of waiting for the sea hawk spread along the line of hunters.

It was midmorning before they sighted two ospreys over the most northerly estuary. A whisper passed down the line: *Now the evil has doubled*. The men and boys surged forward, more avid than ever for the kill. With no knowledge of how the land connected or which channels of water could be crossed on half-submerged sandbars, it was noon before they managed to draw within range of the distant estuary. The commotion they raised in their progress was duly noted by the sharp-eyed hawks. The birds wheeled up and away. With swift powerful wing thrusts they returned to the first estuary and resumed the hunt.

Nothing was left to the thwarted men but to retrace their steps. By the time they reached the line they had held at dawn, the hawks had disappeared completely. Nor were the men rewarded for an afternoon spent scanning the sky. At sunset they returned to the village unaware that watchful eyes had followed them all day.

On that same morning, before dawn, when Siri was preparing to set out for the cliff top, he had scanned the dark land below and noted that the boats again had not put out to sea. When the flicker of lanterns streamed out of Chelney's landward side and moved off toward the estuaries, suddenly he knew the purpose of this day for the men of the village. He forgot about the cliff top, and instead ran down the slope. Today he did not use the Chelney road. Instead, he bypassed the village on its landward side, keeping to the screening growth that fringed the marshland. In this way, unseen, he outflanked the procession of men and boys before it reached the inlet of the first estuary.

Still keeping to the edge of the marshes, Siri found ample cover. The villagers, wary of sinkholes and quagmire, were afraid to walk there. To Siri the way was as clear as the Chelney road. But he did tremble at the thought of the hawks' danger. If they followed the pattern that the male had set, today they would fish the farthest estuary. He had seen them at dawn; the men would surely discover the ospreys as soon as the sun rose. When they did not, he remembered the peculiar sharpening of his own vision. Even from this distance, he could distinguish the scattering of heart-shaped spots on the hawks' breasts, the detail of their rough shanks as they thrust both taloned feet down and forward at the instant of strike on their watery prey. For a moment Siri imagined how this sharpness of vision would serve him if he could truly fly. How wondrous the earth and sea would be! But he pulled his mind back to this day's work. The young on their ledge would perish too, if the parent birds were killed.

When Siri saw how easily the hawks eluded the advancing hunters, he laughed silently in his hiding place among the reeds. But at the end of the day, when the Chelnians gathered together and talked for a long time just outside the village, he frowned and wondered what plan they were making for tomorrow.

During the long day, it came to him that he must think of how he would live. The night before it had been warm, but the weather could change. The cave with its nest would provide shelter in a storm, but a blanket or two would secure him against any sudden cold snap. And he remembered his hunger of yesterday. A small store of salt and perhaps a loaf of the hard, long-lasting bread that the Old Woman baked would be good to have.

Along the edges of the marsh, the tangled berry thickets were loaded with dusky fruit. The supply of fish was endless. Onion bulbs and wild greens of various sorts were plentiful. There were edible roots. Perhaps he could persuade a stray nanny to give up some of her milk from time to time if the boy assigned as goatherd fell asleep. Also, at the edge of the village there was an ancient orchard, now overgrown and neglected, for the Chelnians thought of themselves as fishers and scorned grubbing in the soil. Despite this lack of care, each fall the gnarled trees gave a crop of hard, tart little apples. Then no one in Chelney was too proud to gather the ruddy fruit. It stored well and enlivened their meager diet. Siri decided that this year in September he would somehow manage to secure his share, even if he must pick by moon-light and in secret. All in all, he would do well enough through summer and fall. By then the ospreys would have flown south again. He did not think beyond that.

Yes, blankets and salt, and if he were lucky, a loaf of bread or two. So Siri decided he would risk a final trip home after nightfall when the Old

Woman and Old Man would be asleep. Now he caught a fish from the estuary, took it to the cave and, there perched on the nest, ate it and a handful of berries he had gathered earlier. Then he lay down and slept until the middle of the night.

Chelney was dark when he drifted down through the forested land below the cliffs. It was very late; the old couple would have been in bed for hours. The only light by which to find the way came from a crescent moon and the thickly clotted stars. No wind stirred and the distant sound of the surf seemed only to intensify the stillness. Even the night birds were silent.

Uneasy, Siri stopped some distance from the cottage. He listened for a long time. Nothing stirred in the soft summer night. At last he moved along. When he opened the door to the cottage, he was careful that the latch did not click. With the door closed behind him, he leaned against it. Here he felt safe from any watching eye. Silently he crept through the house. In the lean-to that was his room, he took the blankets from the bed. He closed his mind to the memory of the safe years here when the Old Woman was not so old and her heart not yet hardened against him.

In the kitchen he found the cupboard where she kept the bread. His hand was on the first rough loaf when a tick of sound creased the silence. He froze, motionless, and drew in upon himself. With his own body and breath stilled, noises filled the night. A breeze brushed beneath the eaves. The surf continued on the shore. A village dog barked, off on some distant midnight chase. A mouse scraped along the wall yonder. A mouse? *No.* A movement of cloth against cloth. A whisper of exhaled breath. The creak of muscle over bone.

The little buck rabbit leaped in Siri's mind. With the same terror he bounded for the door. He had closed it; now it stood open. Shadows moved there, blocked his way. Each fiber of the boy's body strained for the safe wild open land. *Too late. Too late.*

A match flared. Lamps sprang to life. Men laughed as they crowded into the little kitchen, their heavy hands on Siri's shoulders and arms forcing him before them.

"A bad day, but a good ending!" one said.

When the Old Man spoke, his voice was smug with his own wisdom. "I told you. An empty belly brings them home. This one has always been hollow to the heels."

The Old Woman, slack in her nightgown, peered from the bedroom door. She squinted against the light and said sourly, as though to console herself, "At least he is safe, the wicked boy." And it came to Siri that she could have warned him but had not.

Yet his tears of rage were at himself. No wild thing would walk so blindly into a baited trap. He tried to twist away from the men who held him. Their hands tightened, wrenching his arms behind him. They were amazed at the strength in the skinny body. It took a brutal effort to subdue him. Siri cared nothing for that pain, but the men's laughter cut through flesh and nerve and bone.

"Oh, those black looks!" Sunderman's voice was hearty. The little eyes, jubilant with success, stared down at the prisoner. "Stop struggling, boy! We'll lock you up until morning. You'll help us then."

But Siri's fierce whisper silenced the laughter. "Chelney can sink in the sea before I'll help you."

Sunderman's looks turned as dark as the boy's. "You'll change that song before we're through. Any who does not work for the good of Chelney works against it. A boy alone cannot slight the common needs. We'll find a way to use you."

The Old Woman spoke uneasily. "You said you'd not hurt him."

Sunderman's voice was hard. "The only hurt he'll get is what he brings on himself. At dawn we'll hunt the fish hawks again and Siri goes with us. Until morning the barred room behind the Meeting House will hold him safe enough."

From a closet, the Old Woman hauled a large muslin sack stuffed with rags. "I have seen that little room," she said. "It has only a stone floor. Let him sleep on this." Then, bitterly, "And give him the blankets he tried to steal."

Alone at last in the cell-like room, Siri went over every inch seeking some way of escape. He could find none. He leaped up and clutched the bars of the small high window, pulling himself up to inspect the way the grid fitted into the frame. It was solid and the screws hard set. Since he had no tool to work at them he dropped to the floor again. Scorning the sack of rags, he wrapped himself in the blankets, huddled in a corner, and tried to sleep. But his mind flew aloft with his hunted hawks. It was not until he imagined himself curled in the nest of needles and leaves inside his cave that sleep finally came.

When Siri awoke, there was no doubt in his mind that he would be able to withstand any pressure the men applied. He would never help to kill the ospreys. He began to think of ways he might hinder the hunt. His plans were carefully made by the time they hauled him from the little room in the early morning darkness.

"You've had a night to think over your evil ways. Today you'll help us," the Old Man growled, and glanced at the other men. He meant they should see he showed no softness to this boy who had been sent to blight his last years.

"The floor was very hard." Siri spoke softly. "Since I couldn't sleep there was plenty of time to think." He did not look at his father, or at Sunderman, who stood above him, or at any of the other men and boys who clustered outside the Meeting House. He was aware that Oren Sunderman grinned at the other boys and nudged the nearest.

"And you *will* help us today." Bartel Sunderman scarcely made it a question.

"Yes," said Siri. "It would be best even for the hawks. If I help, you might have a chance at a clean shot. Then it will be over and done, with no suffering for them." His eyes, flat and dark, flashed to the man's face. Sunderman could read nothing in them.

"You can't believe him." The Old Man sounded suspicious and bitter. "My wife and I have found he talks in circles."

"Have I ever lied to you?" Siri's question sounded innocent enough, and he didn't flinch though he knew he had just answered Sunderman falsely.

"No." The Old Man spoke slowly, for it was so. "It is only that my Old Woman and I think you'll do one thing, but then you do another. You and I look at nothing from the same view."

Siri's voice turned sullen. "Well, then I'll not help you."

His gaze slid to the ground again. Sunderman raised the lantern to better view the boy's face. Since the Council meeting, the man had so convinced himself it was the hawks who had brought these evil times to Chelney that his whole purpose had become the hunt. He burned to destroy the malignant birds. Now he was determined to get the boy's help, for the man was certain that therein lay success.

"Your father was too old when you were born." He put a friendly hand on Siri's shoulder. "He doesn't know how to speak with a young one. Now I myself have three sons and two daughters." He spoke as though this were a great credit to his standing in the world. "So it is clear that I can talk with a boy and come to an understanding with him. Let us make an agreement, Siri, then out we'll go to the tideflats for a good day's hunt together. You and I could become the greatest of friends."

Oren scowled at his father, his eyes resentful

and betrayed. Siri was careful not to draw away from the man's hand. Instead he swung a clear gaze to Sunderman's face.

"We would have to hunt in my way or not at all," he said, his voice as steady as his eyes. "And you would not trust me for that." He shrugged a little.

The weight of Sunderman's hand slid down Siri's thin back to rest in fatherly fashion against the bony wings of his shoulder blades. It took some effort not to twitch away, for all the skin of his body felt sensitive to the harshness around him, and his back itched and burned as though boils sought to erupt there.

Sunderman's hearty voice encouraged him. "Tell me how the hunt should be handled."

Siri looked at him for a long moment before he said, "First we should go to where the hawks will hunt today."

"You are certain of the place?"

"Yes. Unless you so disturbed them yesterday that they changed their habits."

"Where do they hunt today then?" the man asked carelessly.

"I shall show you." Siri's smile was guileless. "But only a few men must come. There is too much movement and noise from so many."

"That's true. Four men will go, and we'll remain hidden until you arrange a clear shot for us."

Siri's smile blossomed. "That is the way it should be done. The hawks are used to seeing me and won't take fright. Besides, I've learned their cries and can call them close."

Now Oren spoke, his voice surly. "He can do that. He sounds like a hawk himself." Then a sudden thought came to him and he said slyly, but speaking so all could hear. "Maybe it's Siri *and* the hawks together that brought a curse on all of us. I've watched him out there all spring, running like a wild wicked thing while the hawk circled above him. It wouldn't surprise me if they flew off together some fine day."

The other boys giggled and nudged each other, but the men looked solemnly from one to another and began whispering among themselves. Though they disliked the Sunderman boy, he had just voiced the thought that crawled at the bottom of each man's mind. They all knew the old myths of half-human birds sent by evil forces to blight the lives of humans.

But Sunderman shook his son roughly by the shoulder. "You make a fool of yourself. See, the other boys laugh at you. As well they might!"

The man was determined not to lose Siri's help.

His position as Leader of Chelney was precarious. Now he felt that the destruction of the hawks would save the village and firmly establish him in a place of honor. No one would ever scoff at him again, and future Chelnians would remember Bartel Sunderman with grateful respect.

With the man's approval of their subdued snickers, the other boys now hooted in open derision. Oren saw that they all were against him. Angrily he turned away and stalked off toward home. Sunderman began choosing the men for the day's hunt, himself and three others.

The Old Man insisted on his right to one of the four places. "After all, despite his wildness, Siri does belong to me," he said.

Siri scanned the sky and said nothing.

5

They had come in a roundabout way to the second estuary. The sky was still dark, but even in daylight the four men would not have noticed that the boy had chosen a devious path. He settled each man behind a grassy hummock, then took his place forward on the exposed sandspit. They would think him imprisoned there with the sea on either side. Yet where the water appeared to them as an impassible barrier, in reality it was shallow in over two-thirds of its distance to the mainland beyond.

Freedom was his on the instant if he wished.

He could splash across and be gone long before
the men realized their stupidity. But freeing himself was only half the plan. The other part was to
show the hawks their danger in hunting here. He
was certain his own escape would be easy for the
men would be afraid to follow him into the dark
region of the cliffs where he would flee. After
today, though, he could never dare enter Chelney
again. It didn't concern him that there would be
no salt, no bread, no blankets or other comforting
things to ease the way. The ospreys survived it all,
and so would he. At this Spartan prospect a fierce
joy seized him.

It was only when he thought of the hawks that
his spirit faltered. They might never trust him
again, yet he accepted that painful sacrifice. The
question that gnawed at his mind had to do with
the real danger. Was the risk too great for the
hawks? Suddenly doubts overwhelmed him. Sup-
pose the men were too quick with their guns. Or
the hawks did not heed that warning shriek he
had learned from them. If fear dried his throat so
that his voice did not carry, or if they hesitated an
instant too long so the men—

Siri snatched his mind from these fears. His
head must be clear and cool, or disaster would sail
in on the wind with the ospreys. He settled to
wait. The morning was not as warm as yester-

day's had been, and the sky to the south was cloud streaked. The chilly breeze dried the fear-sweat on his body. By the time the hawks appeared in the brightening sky, Siri's mind had become lucid and precise again. At first the birds wheeled above the mouth of the estuary where it fanned into the sea. Each made a quick catch; each disappeared to the south. Siri knew that presently they would return. He arose and with seeming unconcern strolled back to where Sunderman was concealed.

"We will fail if you can't keep the men from showing themselves," Siri told him.

He did not say that it was Sunderman himself who had stepped into the open as soon as the hawks had left with their catch. Half angrily the man said, "The hawks have flown. You did something to warn them!"

Siri laughed. "They made a catch and took it off somewhere to eat." He didn't mention the aerie on the cliffs. "Soon they'll return. But the barrel of your gun showed from the cover here. The hawks can see even a mouse from a great distance off, and they're wary."

"I held my gun at the ready for a good shot when they came in." Sunderman was truculent.

"Then don't hold it at the ready unless you plan to shoot only the empty sky." Siri stared steadily into the other's eyes.

The man glowered for a moment, then looked away. Grudgingly he had to admit to himself that what the boy said was true. So he turned his temper on the others. "If you're clumsy enough to show your guns, we'll never get a clear shot!" he bellowed at them.

"Or if the sound of your voice scares the hawks off," said Siri softly.

By the time he returned to his place on the sandspit, it was a certainty the men would keep their guns hidden, unready for any quick action. He had given the hawks every chance he could. Presently the pair came sailing back, made another catch at the estuary mouth, and were gone as quickly as before. This time the men waited quietly. When the ospreys returned and flew in along the estuary, Siri tensed, for he saw that they had spotted him where he sat, silent, in the morning sun. Slowly he raised one hand. The male circled nearer; the female followed.

Since that first time in June, the male had become used to the sight of him. Often curiosity or some strange attraction brought the hawk swooping low. He remembered how, in the beginning when he had first tried to imitate its harsh screaming cries, he had only frightened it away. But as his ear had become attuned to the variations of pitch and the cadence of its calls, the fierce bird began to respond to the cries, slanting in so close that Siri could hear the rustle of the wind in the fanned primaries and the soft whisper in the close feathers of its body. For a brief moment the round golden eyes would look into his dark ones, and sometimes there came the soft chattering call entirely different from either the hunting or warning cries when the hawk was aloft.

Now the female trusted her mate's instinct and flew in close at his wing. Siri blanked the fear in his mind. His thoughts became small precise crystal globes that moved in calm order from one point to the next. He arose. He lifted his hand again. He watched the hawks tilt and begin their descent toward him. With scarcely a movement of his head he checked to see that the guns had not been raised. All safe. For the moment.

Slowly, oh so slowly, he moved away from the men. His gaze was fastened on the hawks. When he heard the small lap of the breeze-driven wavelets, he knew he was almost at the water's edge. A quavering, coaxing cry rose from his throat. The hawks came more swiftly. The beautiful things!

Not too close.

"Now!" cried Siri.

And the hunters—even the Old Man—sprang up, quick as wild goats. Four gun barrels swung aloft. But in that instant Siri gave a great shrieking cry. The men's blood crackled with ice. Their neck hairs bristled. But they managed to fire.

Already the ospreys had pivoted away on a wing tip. The female was only a little slower than her mate. Siri's heart leaped in triumph. He heard the hawks scream in answer to his own cry. He was certain their fierce bright gaze had seen the danger of men and guns. The birds split away from one another and thrust off singly, at first flat across the water for quick speed. Then they whirled aloft.

Siri leaped into the shallow estuary. For the first dozen yards the water was at his hips. He struggled forward against it. Then the sandy bottom rose and the skim of water reached only halfway up his shanks. His high-stepping stride carried him rapidly away. The second volley of guns already seemed distant. Siri continued to run as he scanned the sky for the fleeing hawks.

His heart raced with elation, with release. Not only had he saved the ospreys and himself, but also that hidden thing which seemed like his own soul, that part of him that had flown the skies since summer began. The hawks would never return to the estuaries. And he would never step inside Chelney again. At least this was the promise he made to himself as he ran. For him there would be the wild lands and the dark cliffs, safe from the superstitious villagers. For the hawks there would be the shallow shoals among the off-shore islands where they could hunt in peace. Farther to fly, but not impossible. In this swift moment of escape, Siri banished the thought that the birds might flee the Chelney coast entirely and leave him solitary.

His searching eyes found them. The male was still rising. Smaller and more agile than his mate, he had outdistanced her. She was flying heavily. Siri stopped his own plunging run. It seemed that suddenly his heart stopped also. The female had begun to spiral down. One wing dragged rakishly askew.

Siri felt a terrible pain in his own shoulder. He screamed aloud. Then he was running again, but no longer toward the other shore. He forgot the safe haven of the cliffs south of Chelney. Instead he raced back to the spit of land. Angling off, he gained it before the running men. More swiftly than they, he sprinted toward the narrow end where it jutted into the sea. There the incoming surf struggled with the outflow of the estuary waters. The currents ridged, deep and roiled.

The female osprey could stay aloft no longer. The male had seen his mate's distress. He circled once. Wildly, Siri glanced back at the men. They had stopped running and had lined their guns against the osprey that hung above them in the bright sky. They no longer watched the fall of their first victim. Siri shrieked time after time, that great harsh call of doom. Yet he did not slacken his stride, for there had been a splash in the glittering tide race where the female had fallen. Perhaps she was still alive. But she would drown out there, for the great unwebbed talons were made only for the hunt. It was the wings that snatched the birds from a watery death when they plunged after prey. Wounded, she was helpless.

At least Siri's cries had succeeded with the male, who circled higher, higher, then with a final wild and distant shriek flashed away. The white glimmer of underparts flickered off to the south against the gray clouds. Then he was gone.

At the end of the sandspit, Siri launched himself into the water, struck out for the downed hawk where she floundered in the tide race. Because of his leanness, he had no buoyancy. Yet desperation and his stringy strength carried him through the wicked currents. He had had little fear when he climbed the cliffs, and none when he threaded the boggy estuary land. But water was not his element. The sucking whirlpools terrified him. Yet he plunged ahead.

As Siri swam, he saw the hawk's good wing point to the sky. It flailed time after time, trying to lift the brave bird into the air. She made no sound that he could hear. There was only the wing, flagging her will to stay alive. She disappeared again and again, rolled under by the rough surf. But each time there was the wing, and each time Siri was nearer.

He had not thought of how he would save the fierce bird, but when he finally reached her, she was half drowned and did not struggle against him. Siri managed to grab the good wing close to the body. Its great strong humerus bone was solid in his hand. But the wounded wing dragged and made progress slow. All the bulk of the bird was in those wings, and the lightweight body impeded them not at all. She was too stunned to fight him. He was too desperate to fear the powerful curved beak or rapier talons.

The men gathered on the strand. They were fascinated by the struggle of the boy, and therefore neither helped nor hindered. When Siri pulled himself and the hawk ashore they drew back a little, still watching, still silent. It was clear to them that the hawk was finished. If by some miracle it did survive, they knew they could complete their work anytime they chose. For the moment it satisfied them to watch what the boy would do. Only the Old Man looked uneasy. Perhaps he was glad the Old Woman was not here to see this. He did not like to have her unhappy and he knew she would suffer over the callousness of the men.

Siri ignored them, and only did what could be done from moment to moment. He acted as though there were still hope for the hawk and for himself. Her eyes were glazed, but presently she revived somewhat, then regurgitated water and half-digested fish. She shook her head and feebly tried to right herself from where she lolled in the sand. When Siri handled the hurt wing she drew her neck back, hissed a little, half lunged at him, the hooked beak only mock fierce, for, surprisingly, she withheld the strike.

He spoke to her softly as he inspected the wound. It made him wince to see it. The large bone was broken cleanly near the shoulder, but the feathers and flesh were torn and bloody along the leading edge. He guessed the shot that had mangled muscle, tendon, and feathers had only cracked the bone; the sudden plunge into the water had snapped it rather neatly in two. Siri was sure that if he had her alone he could save her. But the men hung above them like vultures. He glanced about. He thought of evading the men, making a run for it. It was possible he might outdistance them alone. But to do that he would have to abandon the hawk.

Slowly he removed his shirt and began to tear it into strips. Ignoring the threats the hawk made with beak and talon, he bound the broken wing against her body. With the pain eased, she again tried to lift herself into the sky with her good wing. She toppled over and the men laughed. Despite the ignominy of her position, she gazed at them with fearless dignity. Siri righted her. Once more she made the rapid tearing pass at his hands. But she did not touch him, though he knew she could have. Again she tried to fly and fell; again the men laughed. When Siri set her on her feet for the third time, she made no further effort.

"It is enough." The Old Man spoke without expression. He was the only one who had not laughed. He raised his gun. "Move aside, Siri." The words were flat, but not unkind.

The boy spread himself between the hawk and the Old Man. "How can you kill such a brave bird?" he cried.

His eyes, black and round, stared as fearlessly as the hawk's. His bare chest heaved with the stormy beating of his heart. The Old Man noted how the ribs had narrowed and thrust forward, how the arms were nothing but sinew and bone, how the shoulder blades stood almost separate from the body. He supposed it had something to do with lack of good food. Perhaps the Old Woman would be able to persuade the boy from his wild ways, for certainly the men would haul him back to Chelney. It was clear he had tried to thwart their plans; the other hawk had escaped entirely. The Old Man wondered uneasily what penalty the villagers would exact from the boy.

"Stand aside," the Old Man said again. "Don't you see it is kinder to finish with this quickly?" But his temper rose when Siri did not obey him. In bitter anger the man cried, "You are truly a curse upon me!"

It was Sunderman who laughed. "Such impatience, Old Man. Do not shoot the hawk."

For an instant there was hope in Siri's heart. The men looked at Sunderman in surprise. But the next words destroyed the boy's hope, though the men decided that perhaps they had misjudged Sunderman all along.

"We aren't concerned about the fish the hawks have taken in their hunting." Sunderman spoke reasonably as though instructing ignorant men. "When good fortune was with us there were enough fish so we would not have missed those few. It is that the hawks are evil. Remember, one day our hatches were full, the next it seemed no fish were left in the sea."

He paused a moment to give them time with this idea, then went on. "It is obvious. The Devil's curse has been called upon us. And this one," he pointed at the hawk, "and the other that got away are surely the Devil's servants."

He rubbed his chin and his little eyes became wise. "We can thank Siri for the small bit of fortune we had today. Without him we'd not have captured even one of the hawks." He began to smile, for he was pleased with the idea that had come to him. Softly he asked, "Do you not remember how in all times past men have dealt with Satan's servants?"

Suddenly Siri saw what awful plan Sunderman was turning in his mind. The Old Man scowled, but one of the others said, "The torch! Witches and the like must be destroyed by fire!"

Sunderman chuckled, nodded. "Now you see how this day must end. A bonfire tonight and all the village will come. Bring the fish hawk along, but carefully," he ordered. "And the boy. We will have him set the torch. With a little training, Siri will yet become a useful man in Chelney." And craftily he trapped the boy with his next words. "His help will prove that my son Oren was wrong. If Siri lights the fire to destroy the Devil's bird, why then it shows he's innocent of evil himself."

The Old Man turned away and silently stalked off along the sandspit. Sunderman followed, pushing Siri before him. The boy did not let the sick fear in his heart show in his eyes or face. His mind was already busy, seeking some way to save the hawk. But there seemed no exit from this trap.

The other men trailed behind; one of them warily carried the hawk. He had fashioned a hood from his kerchief and slipped it over the bird's head so the wicked beak would not tear his hands.

PART THREE

The Ospreys

6

It was silent within the cell. When Siri moved, the hawk's gaze followed him. Her head swiveled, otherwise she hunched there motionless. He could read nothing in the black-masked, yellow-gold eyes. She only watched and waited. But then, she had no knowledge of what was to come. He envied her this.

Earlier, Siri had heard the people of the village as they gathered wood and built a pile of it in the open space behind the Meeting House. Their laughs and shouts made it seem they were preparing for a festival. Perhaps they saw it thus. Tonight's work would rid them of at least half of the Devil's curse.

They had begun to look to Sunderman as a real leader. It was he who had defined the evil, he who had already captured one hawk. In a few days, surely he would snare the other. So ardently did they desire a leader who would relieve them of uncertainty and blame that they shut their minds to the thought of his bullying ways.

"After all," they said, "Sunderman has brought that rebellious Siri to heel. A good example to all our young people." For there was not one of them who did not worry that his children might harbor secret thoughts of one day going an independent way. Already a few young couples had left the village and not returned. And some of the more defiant boys who served aboard the boats cast black looks at their elders from time to time, resisting their dour and autocratic ways. "Yes, a good example," the men repeated, and gave each other knowing looks.

While the people enjoyed themselves constructing the pyre, Siri again went over the cell inch by inch. Escape seemed as impossible as before. But when he pulled himself up by the bars of the high window, the button at the waist of his ragged pants grated against the wall. He dropped to the floor again, inspected the metal disk, then wrenched it loose. He owned no belt and with the button gone, the pants were too large for his thin hips. They slid down about his ankles. With no hesitation he stepped out of them, leaving himself naked in the chilly room.

The morning had not been warm, and as afternoon advanced, more clouds had crept up from the south. Now their spread extinguished the sun. The cell darkened. Siri shivered, but he snatched up the shucked pants, leaped again to cling to the iron grate. Deftly he slipped one pant leg through the bar, knotting it with the other to form a sling. He thrust one foot through the loop, and thus supported he inserted the thin edge of the metal button into the slot of one screw head. The round disk gave poor leverage. It took him several minutes to coax the screw into a half-turn, then another. After that it went more easily. But there were two screws to each side of the rectangle. Seven more screws. Quickly he calculated. At least another half-hour's work. And the afternoon was waning.

Panic painted a terrible scene in his mind.

. . . darkness . . . time for the fire . . . they are here . . . they take the hawk, then drag me out . . . a torch is thrust in my hand . . . Sunderman laughs and puts the osprey on the pinnacle of the piled wood where the flames will take longest to reach . . . he orders me to set

the torch . . . I resist! . . . oh, how I fight them! . . . I scream, "never, never!" . . . they are all laughing . . . other hands start the blaze . . . they force me to watch . . . the flames and the hawk . . . the hawk . . .

He snatched his mind from the terrible thoughts.

All the while, the osprey, safe on the floor below, had continued to watch him. Now he spoke softly to her and she raised her short crest, ruffled the feathers of her good wing and neck, drew them close and sleek again, and returned to her fixed gaze. Despite his own cold nakedness, Siri glistened with sweat. Again he began to work feverishly at the screws. The work was infinitely slow, and in his desperation he bent the button. This made the task almost impossible, but still he continued. His fingers were bleeding, and only three of the screws had been removed when he heard voices outside the door. With his concentration broken, it surprised him to find that he was silently crying.

One voice belonged to the Old Woman, and there was a man's grumbled reply. It had not occurred to Siri that they would set a guard at the door.

The Old Woman sounded outraged, querulous. "Surely they don't mean to starve the boy."

"No one starves in a few hours," the man answered. "And I was told not to let even one person in."

"Who knows when he last ate?" she insisted. "You saw him. He scarce looks like a human child any more. A wind would blow him away."

"He looked tough as whipcord to me."

"There can be no harm in letting me take this bit of food in," she urged.

"Sunderman said—"

"Sunderman! If he has his way he will rule every life in Chelney. Does he already rule yours? Think how it will be when you have to ask before you dare do any private thing that nature demands."

She gave a harsh, raucous laugh. The man laughed also. Siri quickly untied the pants, dropped to the floor with them, yanked them on, and settled among the rumpled blankets still piled in the corner.

The Old Woman pressed the advantage that the laugh had given her. "You can guard the door closely while I go in and out. No harm will be done. There's little affection between the boy and us. Still, one does not let a child go hungry forever. You have a son near Siri's age. Would you let him go without even a little—" And from the sound of her voice the torrent of words could have gone on forever.

"All right, all right," the man groaned. "But if Sunderman comes, it is you who will have to explain to him." Then there was the rattle of a key in the door. A rift in the thickening clouds let the last of the sun's rays slice through the opening as the Old Woman slipped in.

She stood blinking in the gloom. A sharp breeze with a smell of coming rain had swept in with the instant of sunlight, and the hawk stirred. It was this movement that caught the woman's eye. Some cold curiosity drew her to it. She bent above the bird. It hissed softly and drew its head back, glaring with its hard pale eyes.

"Wicked thing," the Old Woman muttered. "No wonder Sunderman convinced them that Satan sent you."

Then she saw Siri in the dark corner. She set a small wicker basket in the middle of the floor. "There's some food for you." Her voice sounded uncertain, her hands rasped together, paper dry. "Maybe it will help you through this evening."

"I'm not hungry." He peered at her from where he crouched.

"No. Not hungry," she agreed. "But empty. Emptiness is more difficult."

It surprised him she would know the difference. Perhaps he'd never be hungry again, but the hollow feeling was truly hard to endure. When the Old Woman continued, the words scarcely crept across the room to him.

"There is something else in the basket. A couple of fish for the bird. You must love the creature to have risked yourself so. The Old Man told me."

Then they only stared, each studying the other, until the silence grew unbearable. Finally Siri whispered, "It was good of you to bring the fish. For the hawk I thank you."

Presently she muttered to herself, "I don't like to think of this night," and started for the door. She said over her shoulder, "There is something else there that might serve a purpose." Then she was gone, and the key rattled again in the lock.

Siri scuttled to the basket. When he looked inside he found the fish neatly wrapped to keep the wetness and smell enclosed. He tossed one fish to the hawk. She looked at it intently for a moment, then started to tear it apart, gulping ravenously. There were two meat sandwiches made with the coarse dark bread the Old Woman baked herself. And a small slab of cheese and an apple, a little shriveled from long storage. He knew she must have thought awhile about the meat and cheese. They were hard to come by. She and the Old Man usually ate fish, and never both meat and cheese at the same meal. Siri wondered at her generosity now, and at the risk she had taken to help him.

Quickly, though, he set the food on the floor, ran one hand around inside the basket. He could scarcely believe it when he brought forth a battered screwdriver. The Old Woman had said last night that she had seen the inside of this room. It amazed him she would have remembered the barred window and thought of the only thing that might set him free.

In seconds he was settled at the grating again. Outside it was almost dark. His heart raced. His chest hurt with each breath. The screwdriver made escape truly possible. This new hope increased his terror. The work went quickly, but Siri felt caught in a nightmare, each move leaden, evil swiftly overtaking him. In reality it was only a matter of minutes until he had removed all of the screws but one. He loosened this last one, but left it in place to hold the bars until the final moment.

Unknotting the pants, he dropped them to the floor, then slithered down himself. With the shift of weight, the single screw gave, slipped, but held. He did not notice. The hawk must be secured so he could carry her. And there was also the food. He was shaking violently, so he wolfed down one of the sandwiches. Then he retrieved the pants, tied a knot in the ankle of one leg, put the cheese, the remaining sandwich, and apple in this pouch, then tied another loop above the stash. Next he knotted the other leg close to the crotch so that the body of the pants formed an open-mouthed sack.

He tried to ignore the sounds that filtered in from outside. The villagers were gathering for the evening's spectacle. Soon there would be the key in the lock, and Sunderman would come to take the hawk for the beginning of the awful festivities.

Frantically, Siri tugged at the stiff lacing of the wicker basket. It cut into his fingers, but he was able to wrench one end loose. Swiftly he unlaced it until he had freed a two-foot length of cord. This he threaded through the belt loops of his pants. He dropped the remaining fish into the seat of the trussed garment and held it toward the hawk. For a moment she hesitated. Then, her huge appetite unappeased by the one fish she had eaten, she thrust her head forward for this other. Deftly Siri scooped her into the makeshift sack. For an instant she fought him. Quickly he cinched the waist tight, drew it down above her, secured it with the drawstring he had fashioned. In the close gloom she became as calm as a hooded falcon.

The sounds from outside had grown steadily louder. The people were gathered near the great pile of wood. Their voices rose with laughter and harsh chatter when Sunderman appeared. All had forgotten that they had once scorned him as small-minded and a bully. His arrival signaled the start of the evening's ritual and filled them with a dark excitement.

In the cell, Siri was ready for flight. He had tied the pant legs across his chest so the hawk in her sack rested snugly against his back. This left his hands free, ready to grab the bars, pull them both up. Next unlatch the window, slip one hand behind the loose grate, and use the outer sill for a firm hold. A wrench of the grid and the final screw would snap. Then freedom would almost be theirs. From the niche of the window he would watch for a safe moment, drop to the ground, and escape in the gathering twilight. It was a good plan, one that would work. But without the screwdriver all would have been lost. He thought of the Old Woman and was sorry no soft words had passed between them.

Below the window, he prepared to leap. Then with horror he saw that the grate hung at a rakish angle above him. There had been that slip of the anchor screw when he had slithered down. If he sprang up and grabbed the bars, his own weight, with even the slight addition of the hawk's, might wrench loose the sagging frame. There was no way to gain the high window without the bars for a handhold. He slipped the sling from about his chest. Frantically, on hands and knees he searched the floor for the screws he had thrown away. He tried to shut the sound of the approaching crowd from his mind.

An eternity passed before he found one screw. In his nakedness and fright he shuddered from head to toe. Now the screwdriver. He leaped for the window. The grid almost jarred from its one mooring as he swung up. He thrust his right arm behind the metal frame, unlatched the window, pushed it open, then secured a firm hold on the sill. Supported in this way, he tightened the loose screw with his left hand, thrust the other screw in the hole above, set it, twirled it in place, tightened again. Now the bars held steady as he clung to them for an instant before he dropped to the floor once more. Sunderman's voice was outside. The man bantered with the crowd that had followed him to the front of the building. He reveled in the people's approval.

"The key, man, the key," he cried to the guard, expansive and jovial.

Inside, Siri again slipped the sling over his shoulders, settled the muffled hawk against his back. He crouched below the window. The jangle of keys outside launched him upward. His exertions and his terror had weakened him. Even with only the modest weight of the osprey—much of her bulk was feathers—he barely reached the grating, clung, pried it open, found a solid hold on the sill. He wrenched at the grid's open edge. The leverage and his own frantic efforts bent the old screws. They snapped and the frame clattered to the floor. The talk and laughter from outside covered the sound. There was the scrape of metal on metal as the guard set the key in the lock. Siri swung his legs over the window ledge, flung the screwdriver far out into the night so no one could guess that the Old Woman had helped him. No time to see if all was clear, yet fate had gathered every man, woman, and child of Chelney at the front of the building. All but one. The Old Woman had returned to her cottage and shut the door and her mind against this terrible night.

Siri hung by his hands for an instant, dropped; inside a click as the guard succeeded with the key.

Sunderman was regaling the people. "It's dark enough to begin now. Tonight will rid us of half our curse. Tomorrow Siri will help us secure the other hawk."

"Perhaps," someone said, "but the boy is a mulish one."

Sunderman's voice hardened. "This evening will subdue him. You will see. It takes a wise head to know how to handle a rebellious boy like Siri."

But when he and the others entered the cell, they found it empty. The villagers drew back in superstitious fear at the hawk's evil power. Or had Oren been right? Was it Siri himself who had worked this dark magic? As they whispered, each to the other, their certainty grew that the outcast boy and the hawks worked together for the destruction of Chelney.

When Sunderman saw the iron grate lying on the floor, he muttered, "Cursed Devil's child. How did he manage that?"

Although the people were relieved to see the escape was accomplished by common means, Sunderman's fear sprang up again. The men might blame him for the loss of the boy. They had begun to trust him, but he knew they could change as easily as the tide and snatch the leadership from him. Without that, he was nothing. But fear lent him cunning and he spoke quickly to divert the murmuring villagers.

"The boy can't go fast or far. Remember, he carries the hawk. Spread through Chelney and round about. We'll find him and drag him back. We've been too easy on him. Oren was right after all. Surely the curse that has fallen on Chelney can be blamed on Siri *and* his hawks. Those evil birds are the boy's familiar spirits, that is clear."

Then suddenly he saw a way to be rid of Siri for good, and at the same time quiet the people's dark fears. So, carefully, he planted the seed. "When we have our hands on him again, consider, perhaps the fire should serve a double purpose."

But all of this had given Siri a little time. Alone, he was swift as the wind, but burdened by the injured hawk, there was no hope he could outdistance any who might follow. Only stealth could save him tonight. He was grateful for the clouds that had engulfed the stars. But presently it was evident that the rising storm might soon betray him. Distant lightning forked quick as a snake's tongue, and the uneasy rumble of thunder rode up the southern sky.

7

At first the hunt went badly. As rain began to fall, the scattered groups of men freely cursed Sunderman for sending them out in a storm. They had rushed to block the fugitive's way toward the cliffs. The thought of those heights terrified them, and now they were certain they had the boy trapped somewhere in the fields and thickets near Chelney.

The thunder increased and presently shook the sky from rim to rim, flattening the land below. With each slash of lightning, the countryside quivered in dazzling clarity. When the men began to sight their quarry from time to time in the erratic sheeting brilliance, they became elated with their good judgment in cutting off the boy's escape. Each view was a still scene captured by flash; the latest, Siri atop a fallen log. He had whirled to look at the men. They were no more than fifty feet away, rooted for an instant in the blinding strike that revealed the naked boy. His eyes stared wide and wild; his cockscomb of hair bristled, untamed by the rain; his gaunt body and long legs spraddled in transfixed motion for the blazing second. Then all plunged into darkness and the men, too late, rushed forward, collided with one another, shouted, cursed.

A breath later, the next bolt revealed Siri's pale buttocks and heels as he dived into the thick growth that here edged the marshes. This time, the men forgot their fear of quicksand or quagmire and pressed in mad pursuit.

"He has that wretched bird in the sack," shouted one. "I'd wager my boat—"

"Bare as a stripped sapling, he is! Crazy or cursed—"

"After him!" "Circle left, right—" "He can't run fast lugging that thing—" "We have him now—" they encouraged one another.

Their shouts gathered other clots of running men. Only the intermittent thunder blanked the noise they made. But Siri, silent, continued to elude them. The men forgot their anger at Sunderman. Enthralled with their hunters' lust, even the increasing wind and rain did not quench their avid, cruel intensity. Each panted to be the one who would seize the prey. They forgot that Siri had ever been a child of the village. The men whooped in their strange ecstasy as they chased the wild fleeing thing.

Siri ran and dodged and hid and ran again. He tried once more for the safety of the cliffs, but almost collided with a trio of hunters. The dark hid him, but dreading the next lightning strike he angled back and toward the estuaries. Even he did not dare the deep swamp at night. Beyond the thorny fringe where he had first hidden, quagmire or sinkhole awaited. He worked toward the open land, ready to flatten with the next flash of lightning. But when it came, it proved a friend. Without it he would have blundered headlong into a dozen men that Sunderman had rallied to him. Yet in that same instant they saw him, too.

Here the land gave no cover. His only hope was the estuary directly ahead. He fled straight for the water that boiled and foamed beneath the wind and slashing rain. Squall-driven surf boomed far off to the right. The men streamed behind him. Each flare of light showed that slowly they gained. Siri could no longer guard the hawk's safety. He felt her body bumping against his shoulders as he ran. Still, he would not discard her.

There was no place for him to escape but directly into the rising water. He plunged in, struck off in the dark toward the estuary's mouth. It was difficult to swim burdened by the hawk, but dimly he knew that if the men failed to see him within the first few minutes he had some chance of escape. With any distance between them, his dark head would be lost to view in the water's chop. They'd not guess he swam out toward the killing surf and would extend their hunt to the other side of the estuary.

Even in his extremity, Siri planned his way. Risk the tearing surf, come to land on this same side of the inlet. While the men searched to the north among the tideflats, he would cut back through the fringe of Chelney, along the jetties of the harbor, then south to the cliffs. If the hawk survived this terrible night, perhaps she would live and heal on the ledge of her own aerie.

As the cold water rose about his shoulders, the swaddled osprey came to life. In her frantic effort to escape the sudden immersion, she thrust her talons through the worn cloth into Siri's back and there she clung, unable or unwilling to loose herself. The agony almost forced a scream from him. No longer was he aware of the men. The warring currents seized him; blindly he bore to the right. Sometimes vortex or eddy snatched him under; sometimes he swam freely in an unexpected calm. Too numb to care when finally his knee hit the sandy bottom, he stumbled ashore, and with no pause started southward.

Presently Chelney loomed before him. The lurching lights of the fishing fleet marked the little harbor where the boats rode out the storm. His back burned from the wounds left by the hawk's talons. She had slowly relaxed her terrible grip and he wondered, dumbly, if she had died. At first the blood had run in warm rivulets down his water-slicked back, but as he dried, it congealed and drew stickily together. The storm rumbled off toward the north, and though the air had cooled for a bit, now the July warmth began to return.

It was not until Siri entered the curve of harbor where the jetties thrust out and the boats were tied to their moorings that his mind began to function. With a dull shock he saw that some disaster was at work on one of the hulls. Despite the recent downpour, fire licked from the portholes of the vessel and had begun to climb the rise of the mast. Already the cross timber was ablaze. That sight, limned against the clearing sky, would be plainly visible across the tideflats. Nothing would bring the men back to Chelney so quickly as a threat to their fleet of boats.

For the moment the harbor area was deserted. But Siri forced himself to a faster pace. He wondered how long that fiery cross had been visible from the estuaries. Even as he questioned, there was the faint babble of voices as the men came streaming into the far end of the village. Siri broke into a lope. The flames of the burning boat cast his own shadow before him. The cockscomb of hair, the bulk of the bundle on his shoulders as he hunched against it, the length of leg, even the motion of those large feet as he ran, for an instant made it seem a great dark osprey flapped along the ground before him. The grotesque shadow led him beyond the perimeter of the village of Chelney.

Some vitality returned to him now. He faced about for a moment and stared at the flames. He had not noticed before and it was hard to tell from this distance, but it seemed that it was the Old Man's boat that burned. As Siri turned back to continue on the way, a movement caught his eye. There, standing alone on a slight rise of ground, was the Old Woman. She was watching the fiery boat and the shadowy silhouettes as the returning men swarmed out along the jetties. In the same moment she became aware of the boy. For a breath of time they each stared into the other's face. There was a flicker of consternation in the Old Woman's eyes. Then as she looked more closely, this changed to horrified dismay. Quickly she turned away and hurried off in the direction of home. In her hand she carried a metal can. It bumped hollowly against her knee.

Siri remembered the can from the days of his childhood. It held the fuel with which the Old Woman had always filled the lanterns that lit the cottage.

The thunder and lightning had rolled away to the north by the time Siri reached the cave. It was too dark to see the hawk when he loosened the sack from about her. He thought she must be dead. But free of the confining cloth, she moved beneath his hand. She was obviously subdued and listless, and he wished there was some light so he could examine her more closely. He felt for the fish in the sack. She had not eaten it, probably because of the close darkness. The rain had kept the fish cool and moist. When he smelled it the freshness was still there. But the hawk would not take it from him. He slipped a loop of the cord about her legs so she could not wander away while he slept. The bandage he had made for her wing was still in place.

Since nothing further could be done until morning, Siri curled in the nest. He ate the apple, then the rest of the food, soggy from the rain and the sea. His pants were also soaked, so he remained naked. His back throbbed where the osprey's talons had scored it, but he shut his mind to this and settled more closely into the leaves and pine needles, drawing his knees against his splayed ribs, wrapping his arms about himself. He ran his hands over the rough scabs where the blood had dried, and further along his sides and shoulders and arms. He felt what seemed to be a scanty hirsute covering there, a new discovery for he paid little attention to his own body. At first this find disturbed him, but then dim memory came of how the Old Woman had fondled him so long ago and traced the downy growth along his spine, smoothed the fine fuzz on forearms and shanks. A baby's bloom. *My little dove,* her whisper drifted down the years.

Now, though, the growth he smoothed was a coarser one. So he further reassured himself with the thought that the Old Man's chest and back were covered with a mat of springy gray hair; it was right that at fifteen he should start a manly crop of his own. Fifteen. No one had thought of his name day this year, toward the end of May; he had forgotten it himself. But then his thoughts

105

changed and presently he laughed softly there in the night, remembering how he had eluded all the men of the village. That pyre of wood was soaked and useless now.

He was very warm and comfortable, and sleep began to take him. Before he finally slipped away, he noticed that the beat of his heart was quick and light and wonderfully fast. Because of it he felt buoyant, and the dark ugliness of this day was forgotten as he fell asleep. He dreamed he flew with the ospreys. They slanted across the estuaries, skimmed past the dark cliffs, then rose higher and began to wing toward the south. This time there was no terror in the flight. Yet presently, in the dream, he wheeled away from the ospreys and back to circle above a village that lay below. All was revealed to his hawk's eyes, now turned miraculously sharp. Then his sleep became dreamless and empty until dawn.

When he awoke he found the female osprey had died in the night. She lay on her side, her talons curled like loose fists. Her golden eyes were closed. She had already begun to stiffen.

8

The stunted pine clung to the cliff's rim. Bent landward by the constant wind from the sea, it had thrust its roots deep within the crack. Siri knelt there and inspected this fissure that strung its green line down the sheer face. There were narrow black openings in the green where the soil had washed away. A few knotty shrubs were wedged at intervals, but for most of its length, down to the overhang, the line was sketched by grasses, thin and insubstantial in the scanty soil.

The dead osprey rode in the makeshift sack of yesterday. The villagers would find no feathered body for the satisfaction of their pyre. He was determined to see the young ospreys, and it seemed fitting that the female be returned to the aerie. The sun felt good against the shadow of growth that covered his body, and he thought nothing of his nakedness. The storm was gone entirely. With nothing to fear from Chelney on these heights, Siri gave his full attention to the task at hand. Carefully he began the descent.

The roots of the pine reached twenty feet down the crack. Where its tough sinews protruded, the holds were secure and he descended easily. There was none of the momentary fear he had felt the other day on the ledges; nor was he disturbed by the awkward bulk of the dead osprey that rested once more on his shoulders. Where the roots ended, soil had collected in the crack. When this was scooped away, a series of solid holds was revealed.

Siri continued down and presently, pausing to rest, he saw that a hundred feet of the descent had been accomplished. Now, though, the split narrowed and the angle of the outer rock face had exposed this fracture to the periodic sluice of rains, which had washed it clean of earth and eroded any holds that might have existed at one time. But Siri jammed fist and elbow, knee and ankle and foot into the crack, and thus persisted in the descent. The whole thing was made possible by short rests on the widely spaced obstinate shrubs that had somehow sprouted in scant splits and depressions where they had collected their own store of soil as they grew.

At last Siri reached the upper bulge of the overhang. It was then he saw the male osprey. The hawk came in straight from the sea, talons sunk in a fish, perhaps caught among the island shoals. Had the tragedy of his mate yesterday warned him of the fatal danger of the estuaries?

Now Siri heard the young ospreys. But the overhang still hid them. The arrival of food had excited the fledglings and their racket rose to a raucous pitch. With only one parent to supply their needs, they must be ravenous. Siri knew this might force them to early flight. At least he had not missed them entirely. He squatted on the tilted bulge, motionless, until the male slanted away again, making off in the direction of the open water.

Quickly Siri arose, moved with precision across the exposed rocky perch. To the south he could see the ledges where he had found the kittiwakes and their eggs, and where he had tumbled the murre back to her sea. On this southerly end of the overhang he could find no way down to the ospreys' aerie. But at the opposite, northern end, he saw an extension of the crack that had led him here.

He managed the upper bit of this crack and began to work his way into the under edge of the overhang. He clung with fingers, nails, toes. The rock seemed to push him into space. His own and the dead bird's weight pulled at him. Finally there was no way to see his next move. Nor did he dare release his present hold to reach for the safer one he had just quitted. Both advance and retreat were suddenly impossible. Yet he could cling there for only seconds. Panic seized him.

In that dreadful instant he heard a rush of wings, glimpsed the hurtling body of some great bird. The young ones screamed and scrabbled about below. The last of Siri's strength deserted him. One foot slipped on its precarious perch. The yank dislodged his fingers. He spun off, down. By luck or some twist of his own body, the next moment he was snared by the rough edge of a huge disordered mound of sticks. He clung, felt the sticks begin to give way beneath him and somehow managed to writhe to a safer spot. There was one brief view of predatory eyes, bee-tled brow, hooked beak, fearsome talons. Wings buffeted his head and shoulders. Then an eagle launched itself from the aerie, dropped away and down into the void, screaming its rage at the thing that had come between it and its intended prey.

With the eagle gone, the young ospreys immediately recovered from their fright. They eyed the new intruder with some wariness. It was not until he struggled toward the safety of the nest's depression that they each stamped from one foot to the other, shrieked, and together lunged at him. Suddenly, laughing, Siri rolled away, leaped out onto the solid ledge, scurried to its far end. There he stood gazing at the ungainly fledglings. They did not quit their nest to pursue him. Instead they stared with bold eyes, shrieked a time or two, then apparently put him from mind and began to tear at the fish left earlier by the male. Siri, fists on hips, dark eyes alight with some fierce joy, laughed again.

After a few minutes he began to look for a place to dispose of the female's body. There was a long deep cleft at the back of the cave formed by the overhang. He deposited her at the far end and covered her with detritus he gathered from the aerie's outer rim. It was then he noted how nearly fatal his fall had been. Most of the nest was well within a spine of rock that guarded the cave's lip. In one spot, though, the nest had been broken down and a portion of it now extended over the void. Perhaps the break was due to past struggles of the young hawks over the food they shared. Whatever the reason, it was this outcropping of sticks, somehow levered into the mass, that had saved him.

Now he settled, motionless, to watch the fledglings. There were three of them. Probably two females and one male, for the one was smaller than his sisters. He was fierce though, and ably claimed a share of the fish. All were now nearly as large as the old male, and would obviously soon be a-wing. When the fish was finished, they began to hunt through the disordered nest for any fallen scraps. A time or two they stopped to eye him, but soon lost interest for he remained perfectly still.

After a bit, the male returned with another fish, dropped it in the nest, watched its noisy offspring while it rested a moment. When Siri eased himself on the hard rock, the small movement caught the male's eye. The bird hissed, raised its short crest, ruffled its feathers, thrust its neck forward as though to see more clearly. Perhaps it remembered Siri from the estuary days. At any rate, it only shifted a little uneasily, bobbing its head up and down at this intrusion of the high sanctuary. Presently it tilted off into the wind again, made one pass before the aerie, turned a bright eye toward Siri, then sailed away in the direction of the islands.

It was mid-afternoon before Siri began to think of how he would ascend the cliff. The task of gathering food faced him, for he no longer dared risk the Old Woman's kitchen. Suddenly it came to him how she had stood outside Chelney last night with the empty fuel can in her hand. It was surely the Old Woman who had set the fire to draw the men back to the village, away from their hotly pursued quarry. Honest in her own hard way, she had fired the boat she considered, at least partly, her own. It was the second time she had risked herself that day to help him. Yet why that look of consternation and dismay when she discovered him there on the outskirts of Chelney? He shrugged. There was really no way to understand the Old Woman. But then he remembered the distortion made of his own shadow by the leaping flames of the burning boat, and decided that the changes in his face and body had frightened her when seen in that garish glow.

Now, on the ledge, he was not alarmed by the difficulty of finding a route to surmount the overhang. But as the afternoon waned and the air chilled, he became anxious and finally desperate. Hunger gnawed at him. He snatched a strip of fish from one of the outraged fledglings and gulped it down. The young birds had become used to his movements during the day and now seemed to accept him as part of the life on their ledge. The old hawk had bristled at him a few times, screamed once or twice, but though there was still a cold watchfulness in the bold eyes, seemed to be, on the whole, unalarmed also.

By the time it was dark, Siri had given up any thought of leaving the ledge until tomorrow. He curled on the hard stone at the back of the shallow cave. The dead osprey had been buried there in the makeshift sack. Siri, naked, shivered in the thin night wind, and thought of unearthing her to retrieve his worn pants. But it seemed scarcely worth the effort. The material was threadbare and offered little protection. Besides, the down on his body was beginning to shield him as well as any clothing. Still, in the cold before dawn the wind became deadly, the stone unbearably rough. His back began to hurt again where the female's talons had thrust in yesterday. Wrapping his arms around his boniness, he ran one hand there and found the roughness had increased. The gashes were raised in ridges that prickled beneath the probe of his fingers. This, added to a tenderness of his shoulder blades that had plagued him for weeks, became intolerable.

Stiffly he arose, stared out at the dark sea and the night where the sharp stars clotted the moonless sky. Presently, through discomfort or pain or loneliness, he crept along the ledge. At the nest he paused. The hawks seemed aware of him for he heard a subdued chatter and hiss. Or perhaps they dreamed as he did. When, after a moment, he crawled over the nest's rim, the hawks stirred, screamed a time or two, lanced at him with their hard beaks. He turned the blows with bony knees and elbows, shielding himself as best he could there in the dark. He held no illusion that they would have spared him if their efforts had given them the taste of blood. Still, it was only instinct on their part, and in no way like the cruelty of the villagers.

Now he did not move, and after a bit the birds forgot him and went to sleep again. To Siri the nest smelled a little sour, but he had noted during the day that the young ospreys were careful not to befoul it with their own droppings. Their ravenous appetites precluded any leavings of fish that might have rotted. The inner surface of the nest was resilient and softer than the stone had been. Warmth, radiated from the bodies of the birds, eased the pain of his back. Presently he slept.

By the end of the week the young hawks were making tentative efforts at flight, hovering safely over the nest's protection. Awkward at first, each hour they seemed to gain in skill. Still, Siri had not found a way to leave the aerie. He knew there would be no help from anyone of the village; even the Old Woman, when she thought of him at all, would convince herself that the mild weather was right for outdoor existence, and that he was gone through his own choice. Siri's smile was bleak. During the past days he had fared well enough, fighting with the young hawks for his share of the food. Perhaps his own odor had been lost after that first night in the nest with them; perhaps the covering of down on his body in some way obscured from them that he was human. Whatever the reason, he was tolerated.

As the young birds became more able in their flight, they ventured farther and farther from the nest until, at last, they could fly with some of the same boldness as the old hawk. One morning Siri realized that tomorrow or the next day they could be gone. Then the male osprey would no longer bring its catch to feed them; Siri would be left to starve. The long hours he had spent trying to surmount the overhang had proved fruitless. Several times in his efforts he almost fell from the ledge. The small amount of fat beneath his skin was now gone entirely. His bones had grown as light as air. It almost seemed to him that if he fell from the ledge, he would settle to earth so lightly that no harm would come of it. But when he peered over the shelf's rim, far below stood the cruel rocks of the shore with the waves gushing between them. Safety was an illusion; the sea would lap his broken frame from those rocky teeth and swallow him with its salty juices.

Terror wore itself out. Now, calmly, he faced the fact that he would starve. Or he could take that braver, quicker death below. Yet the young hawks were loath to leave the safety of their ledge and it was not until the fourth day of their bolder flights that they found the courage to sail far out over the water. The larger of the females, more brave than her nest mates, flew farther than they, then farther still, off in the direction of the estuaries. This one did not return, though Siri watched for her until dark. The other two spent several more nights in the nest.

At last the old hawk, weary from its long efforts with the ravenous brood, brought fish only three times during that day, and nothing for the evening. Siri scrabbled away one of the fish for himself, then part of a second. These he hid in the coolness of the cleft at the back of the ledge. The next morning the remaining pair of hungry young ospreys took wing and like their precocious sister did not return. Now Siri was alone.

He ate the half portion of fish in midmorning, squeezing the watery juices into his mouth as he had for the past days, for there was no water on the ledge. He forced himself to wait until late afternoon before he tore off a third of the flesh from the other fish and consumed it in several gulps. The rest he would save until morning. That would be the last of it. For most of the day he hunched in the center of the nest gazing out over the endless glitter of the sea. He noticed that the boats of Chelney were at their usual work, seining the waters out beyond the islands and the shoals. Perhaps the fish were running again, and the men had forgotten him and the ospreys and the ill fortune they were accused of bringing.

When it was dark, he missed the warmth of the other birds, though the down on his back and sides and belly was thicker now and covered him like a close glossy garment. When he fell asleep, the dreams of flying returned and he soared more easily than ever before. Was it he or one of the young hawks that plunged into the sea, arose triumphant with a gleaming fish clutched in steely talons? Once he stirred and came partly awake. Even in this half sleep, he felt a sharp stab of regret. If only there had been more time; if only the young birds could have lingered another month or two so the old hawk would have continued to feed them all. With time, anything might have been possible.

In the morning the hot August sun woke him. He retrieved the fish from the cleft. Slowly he ate the last of it. Now he crouched unmoving in the nest. He did not think but only waited.

It was noontime when the old osprey flew in with its catch from the sea. It thrust the fish into the disordered nest after alighting on its rim. For a long time the hawk's round golden gaze studied the creature who brooded there so quietly; then it flew off. Yet at dark it returned.

That night the osprey took to roosting in the aerie again. And each day it brought part of its catch for the one that had not flown as yet.

PART FOUR

The Girl

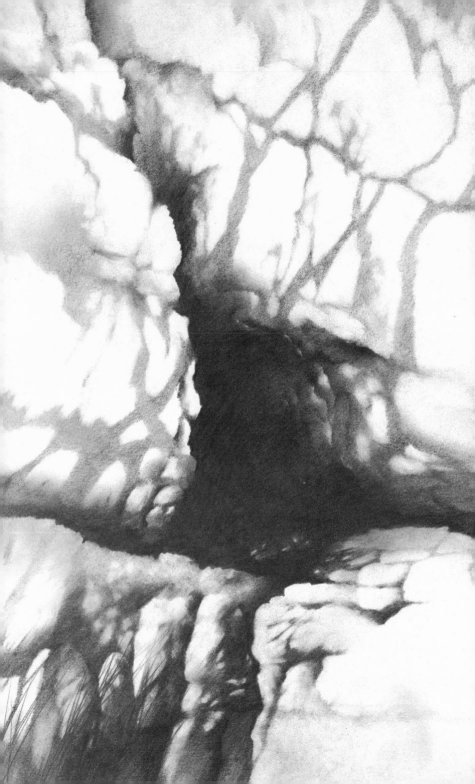

9

Through the end of summer and the month of September the osprey continued to feed the strange fledgling. For Siri, each day hung solitary, a single bead on the thread of time. The wildness spread in his brain and heart and spirit, through his torso, along the tendons, the sinews, the muscles of his legs and feet, of his arms and hands and fingers, and beyond into the air around him.

Sometimes this sense of transition brought a painful tension to mind and body. Then Siri would spring from the nest, pace up and down the ledge time after time. He moved quickly, lightly, but occasionally he stopped to curve and arch his back and shoulders, stretch tall on his long legs, knobby now from the spare diet, and finally to throw his hawk's cry, lonely, piercing, into the wide sky. At last, eased, he would return to the nest to sit motionless, gazing again at the endless sea. Insofar as Siri was concerned, the villagers, the Old Man, the Old Woman, became part of half-forgotten dreams.

Yet as autumn flamed with color, the osprey grew increasingly restless. With winter at its tail, it made tentative flights toward the south. Each time, reluctantly, it returned to the aerie. On this particular day, during October's second week, the hawk was not reassured by the brilliance of the sun. Hoarfrost had glinted in the cold light of last night's full moon. Today a bitter boisterous wind had risen. Along the shore a flood tide was beginning to surge. Already it had drowned the rocky beach, each wave climbing the cliff's base in a frenzy of foam.

As for Siri, even with the close protective down that had thickened on his body since summer, he knew the ledge on this vertical face would soon be untenable. This certainty and the osprey's disquiet drove Siri to a desperate decision. The changes in his arms and back and shoulders, begun in early summer, had continued over the months. If only he could wait a while longer; yet he knew delay had become impossible. He tried to encourage himself with the thought that besides the changes in his upper back and arms, there was the increasing airiness of his bones and the lack of burdening flesh. These differences, that had first disturbed him in July and dismayed the Old Woman so much the night of the fire, he now more stoically accepted.

The schoolmaster who had come to Chelney from outside had attempted to bring to his village pupils some of the excitement of books and learning, of history and language, and the revealed mysteries of science and nature. What he taught had been forgotten by most after Chelney's elders banished him. But the strange and wonderful knowledge, spread before him in those two brief seasons of learning, had fastened in Siri's mind. Now he recalled those times when the man had made friends with him, when together they had explored the estuary lands and had long talks of the things they saw. One discussion had been on the miraculous way in which each creature seemed fitted to live so ably in its own hazardous world. And man, the schoolmaster had told him, was the most adaptable of all living things.

So, on this day, remembering that talk, hope rose within Siri as he noted how the cool, light wildness of his quick heart rocked him, how lean he had grown, how airy the rack of his bones had become. Half wryly he laughed and told himself that his weeks spent hunkered and gaunt in the nest or pacing the confines of this ledge surely must have wrought certain alterations in his body. Of course, he had no way to truly view himself to see if this was so. If he was changed it did not affect the way he now moved with fine precision along the lip of the aerie to scan the surge of the sea so far below. There was his old sure balance, the same easy grace.

Still, during most of this morning he had been filled with terrible indecision, alternately hunched in the nest, perched at the lip of the aerie, or balancing along the length of the precarious rim. Several times he almost launched himself into the gusty void, yet each time his nerve failed him. All the while, the osprey watched with intense un-blinking gaze. Now at last, in midafternoon, with that brief flare of hope, he steeled himself. For a long moment he stood on the edge of the giddy drop. Then despite a spasm of black fear that suddenly erased the hope, he leaped out and away into the murmuring air.

His breath caught. His heart died. He plum-meted down. A strong updraft caught beneath the pinion forms of his shoulders and arms. He tensed the muscles there. Surely, surely the wind would buoy him. His whole being strained to stay aloft.

Dream turned nightmare. No thrust of power. No lifting elation. Though the mighty sweep of currents along the cliff's face sustained him in small measure, the bony projections of his back were insufficient. He spread his body flat, belly down, in the updraft and tried valiantly to guide himself. But the rate of his descent continued unabated. He tilted this way and that, certain at any moment he would dash against the crags, to spin over and down to oblivion. The osprey slanted above, dived below, whirled away and back. In its distress it gave sharp nervous cries.

Finally it was the sea that saved him. The flood tide had reached its peak. Intermittently the surge of breakers rose high against the cliffs. Into this foamy lift of brine Siri plunged, down through the depth of water to crush bruisingly against the rocky shelf of beach. Instantly the receding waves whirled him out, sucked him down into the offshore deeps. The sea swallowed him for an eternity, but at last he rose to the surface, gulped air, struck out for shore. The swim was exhausting for there was no buoyancy in his spare lean body, and those weeks on the ledge had weakened him. At last, though, he gained a jut of rocks, managed to climb above the waves' reach, then lay unmoving. Presently from high above came a hawk's scream. Siri roused, glanced aloft. There the male osprey rose up and up. It flew a dozen climbing spirals, gave a final wild cry, then tilted off toward the south and was gone. A twist of regret turned Siri's heart, but he no longer clung to sorrow as he had when all of Chelney had cast him out. He had been younger, softer then.

He found the cave as he had left it and immediately set about making himself as snug as possible for the coming winter. Last spring's nest of leaves and twigs lay undisturbed. He added to these and provided a base of limber branches. Finally, the scooped couch stood thick and deep at the back of the cave beyond the reach of drafts. Next came the question of food. Thinking of the neglected orchard, Siri stood outside on the steep slope for a long time, gazing down toward Chelney. The memory came of the tart, juicy little red apples. He had lived on fish for too long. Yes, he must chance Chelney. But only before dawn or late at night, and warily, warily.

Early next morning he descended to the orchard. There he managed to gain the treetops where the village children were never able to glean. He laughed aloud, pleased with his success where they had failed. An ample crop of apples still hung there. Perched among the branches, he ate several and found them surpassingly good after the long scant diet with the ospreys.

In the days that followed, Siri continued to scavenge for supplies to carry him through the winter. He even dared return to the cottage once in the dead of night. He took only a few things he would need to survive the arctic cold that would soon sweep down from the north. Next morning the Old Woman was mystified to find that two blankets and an ancient quilt were missing from the linen chest. She did not report this to anyone. Nor did she care that a few worn garments meant to clothe a boy and a battered pair of winter shoes had also disappeared. What use for them with Siri gone forever? So she said nothing at all, not even to the Old Man.

She scarcely understood the impulse that seized her next day. Nevertheless she jammed a bundle of a few useful things into a discarded stewpot, and fitted the lid carefully in place to protect the contents. Making her way south of the village, she toiled part way up the slope there. Afraid to go farther, she set the stewpot in an open space and hurried back the way she had come. When out of curiosity, she returned two days later, the pot was gone. Perhaps some animal had dragged it away, she told herself. But there were no marks in the humusy soil. Since all of this frightened her and she could not bear to think of Siri, she erased it from her mind as well as she was able.

Siri set the stewpot at the back of the cave and forgot it. There were other things to occupy his mind, and he no longer wished to think about the Old Woman's effort at love. Besides, he had no need for anything but the blankets and quilt he had taken. He had lost his taste for cooked food, so the utensils and matches and other things were of no value anyway.

Once it occurred to him that if he did make a fire he could smoke some of the fish so easily caught now. Smoked fish would be useful during the worst of the winter storms when the estuaries froze and the rocks along the sea were festooned with ice. With that thought in mind, he even found a slit in the rock that could serve as chimney to keep the air in the cave clear. Outside, the smoke would disperse in the quick drafts around the cliff's face and not reveal him to the villagers. But then he shrugged. Let the future care for itself.

Still, he did continue to store food. By the end of October, he had a supply of apples and wild onions; he dried sheaves of wild greens he had gathered, leeched acorns of their bitterness in a stream below the hill, and even risked himself raiding a hive of bees he had discovered at the edge of the woods that bordered the marsh. He stored the waxy oozing honeycombs in a scooped erosion of rock near the cave, and picked out the ants when they came and drowned in their effort to rob him as he had robbed the bees. He inspected the little spring that bubbled from a fissure at the back of the cave, arranged a basin of rock that would hold a modest supply of water before it trickled away in its hidden passage.

Once in the night's blackness he was awakened by a storm raging outside. The memory came of the exposed aerie on the open cliffs and he burrowed deeper within the litter of the nest, pulled the blankets more closely about him. Then he smiled, pressed his face into the quilt, and was asleep again.

The S.S. *Laura Ann* had steamed out of her northern port three days ago. She plowed south through the gray seas. There was nothing to mark the voyage as different from the countless others she had made. Her captain scarcely needed his charts to remind him that soon he must set his course farther seaward to avoid the shoals and islands off the Chelney shore. He had commanded the *Laura Ann* for the past decade; he knew these waters better than his own homely face and trusted the crew more than he would have his own family if he had had one.

During the morning of this last day of October, the wind had risen, gusty and turbulent, but at sunset it fell away entirely. A flat sea lay as slick as polished stone. This Judas calm was the undoing of the *Laura Ann.* The quiet air, the still sea lulled the captain's senses. He knew the hardships of the northern harbors, ice-locked in winter, and the sensuous easy life of the warm-water ports to the south. But he had never seen any storm strike with such sudden ferocity as this one on Allhallows Eve. The sky was sweet and clear at sunset. Two hours before dawn the gale blasted down out of the arctic. A roaring sea sprang up, unholy, madly murderous. Two of the crew were swept overboard and lost in the first mountain of water that staggered the *Laura Ann.* The ship's cook, roused from sleep by the pitching of the vessel, hurried to the galley to oversee his domain. The huge coffee pot, forever ready with its hot bitter brew, overturned and badly scalded him. Hurled spray had glazed the rigging, iced the deck. The first mate slipped and broke his left leg above the ankle. A terrified passenger rushed on deck, went down, and cracked his skull. Despite the captain's knowledge of the coast, this series of disasters aboard ship took his mind, for they all had been unprepared for this black storm. Now he had lost his bearings completely.

It was already too late when he heard the hollow boom of surf on the offshore shoals. He could feel the pound of it in his breastbone. The wind and the raging sea drove the *Laura Ann* on the hidden teeth. They ripped her open from stem to stern. The captain's heart went with his ravaged vessel. He had loved her. Still, he kept control of himself and the crew; they all knew their business. They had the half-dozen passengers and themselves in the three lifeboats within twenty minutes, launched in twenty-five.

The captain, not one for heroics, climbed into the last lifeboat. The first foundered almost as soon as it took to the sea. The second managed to clear the lee side of the *Laura Ann*. There it took the full force of the gale, and through bad handling broached to windward and was swamped. It spoke well of the captain's seamanship that he managed to keep his own dory afloat for nearly half an hour, but the maniac sea finally had its way. The currents here ran mostly south. Now these were aided by the force of the northerly, and little flotsam was carried ashore at Chelney. But downcoast they found bits of the *Laura Ann* for months. The sea gave back only three bodies, also in the more southerly waters. The records showed all hands lost.

The *Laura Ann* did not give up her soul easily. At each heave of surf she rose up and tried to tear free. But each following ebb forced her to settle, so the rocks thrust deeper into her vitals. As her wrenched and broken timbers ground against the shoal, she screamed and groaned in the night. During any short respite in the blow, she gave great gusty sighs as water and air sucked in and out of her rendered belly. There seemed no one to hear her monstrous death rattle after the lifeboats were swallowed by the sea. She was almost alone in her agony. Yet not quite alone.

Below deck, the girl remained hidden during the wreck and for the half hour it took the others to abandon the *Laura Ann*. She trembled at the terrible sounds around her. The gut-torn cries of the wounded ship turned her own insides to water. But at first she was more afraid of discovery than death. She waited for the sailor who had smuggled her aboard to come for her. He did not. The passengers were given priority, then, thinking of his own skin, he was the first crewman to crowd into a lifeboat. It was the one earliest launched and quickest lost. No thought of the girl came to him as he struggled, sucked brine, and settled for the last time into the deeps.

When she finally peered out, crept from the locker, and scurried above deck, the girl found herself alone. It was clear that the *Laura Ann* was breaking up on the hidden reef.

She did not grieve for the sailor. When he had seen her ten days ago, he had thought her young and unspoiled. And desperate, for she was little better than scullery maid at the dockside restaurant. There was no one to fend for her and since she was scarcely more than a child, she was at the mercy of anyone who would hire her. The sailor had spoken softly, promising to give her love and a pleasant life, and so had smuggled her aboard the *Laura Ann*. But he had only taken and given her nothing. To build his own slight importance or to keep his fellows quiet, he had shared her with them in the secret bowels of the ship. Despite her youth and the look of purity, she had lost her innocence long ago. She had not really believed his talk of love.

Even with the things done to her here on the *Laura Ann*, the habit of hope was still strong. At least, she told herself, the old life was behind and surely the future would be brighter than the past. For as long as she could remember there had been no ease for her, and only the small pleasures of her own heart had kept her from despair. There was no recollection of her family. They had died or abandoned her in those early years before such memories form. And none had concerned themselves to keep such a record for a wee scrap of girl. Yet silently as she grew, she had held to that hope of better days to come. Even she did not think of this as courage.

Now though, as the planking twisted and groaned beneath her feet, she saw that everything was over for her. Still, the same toughness that had made her struggle so futilely against the crew now made her refuse to die easily. Knowing how the drag of garments and the cold sea could kill in minutes, she rushed to the galley, stripped off her clothes there in the freezing night, smeared herself with a heavy grease. Back on deck, she waited for one of the short infrequent lulls.

As often happens, a bit of luck accompanied the girl's kind of grit, and once, through a rift in spray and clouds, she glimpsed a steady cluster of lights to leeward. A relative quiet followed when only the *Laura Ann*'s gassy sighs filled the air. Not risking a leap into the unknown water, the girl shinnied down a hanging line, slid free on the torn swells which rose to meet her, struck off, away from the lunging side of the *Laura Ann*. She swam strongly, tried to remember the direction of the lights she had seen. But it was a terrible distance to shore.

An eternity later, a white line of breakers thundered before her. The storm had begun to quiet or she would have been dashed to pieces. She had lost all sensation, so scarcely felt the maul of the subsiding waves as they flung her time after time against the unyielding rocks. At last she managed to drag herself above the reach of the sea. In the gray dawn a thin snow began to sift down, for November was the beginning of winter on Chelney's coast.

Siri had fallen asleep, snug in the quilt and blankets, safe from the storm that howled in from the sea. Now the gray early light filtered into the cave and he lay listening to the silence. He arose and outside found that it had begun to snow. Nevertheless he descended to the tide pools and began to search for mollusks or shellfish to satisfy his morning hunger. Just above the reach of the sea he came upon the girl where she had pulled herself onto the rocks. At first he thought her dead. Already a grainy gauze of snow covered her. He brushed it from the pale hair, from the curve of cheek, from the thin skin that covered her eyes. With a thumb he pushed back one of those delicately veined lids. Beneath was only the white turn of eyeball. He wondered where she had come from, then was certain it was from the sea.

138

But on scanning the open water for some sign of vessel, wrecked or afloat, he could see only the thickening veil of snow.

The cold numbed his face, so when he bent to see if some thread of breath came from the girl's half-open mouth he could feel nothing. There was the same frozen insensitivity when he pushed his fingers against her throat. He strained to feel any flutter of pulse. Finally he bent and pressed one ear to her breast. It did not concern him when he found her naked beneath the snow mantle. In reality, he thought, it would have made little difference to him if he had found her dead. His mind seemed as chill as the snow, so it surprised him that his own heart quickened when he heard the stirring of hers.

With no further thought, he picked her up— she was no burden at all—and careful of the icy skim on the rocks, carried her back to the cave. The blankets and quilt were still in their snarl from his own sleep. He spread one, deposited her on it, covered her with the other two, then stood staring down at her for several minutes. Except for the wheaten hair and her pallor, she reminded him of the seals who sunned themselves along the rim of the islands. The water had slicked her hair against her round skull. Her eyes, still closed and lifeless, were set wide apart, nose pointed, upper lip short, upper teeth slightly protruding, a sleek-it soft body, yet strong too. Yes, much like a seal. He wondered if her eyes were brown. And wondered at his wondering. She was an odd creature, he decided, and except for the color of her hair not at all like the solid, stolid girls of Chelney.

Despite the blankets, the pallor did not lessen; her face was translucent, blue around the temples and around the bloodless lips. She remained unconscious. Presently Siri went out from the cave. When he returned a little later he carried a load of broken branches and a fish he had managed to scoop from a pool left by the high rise of last night's storm. He picked up the Old Woman's stewpot, emptied the miscellany of her offering, and filled it with spring water. He set rocks to hold the pot, poked wood beneath, and was glad for the Old Woman's matches to light it. Once the fire was blazing, the split in the rock drew well. When the curve of wall threw a portion of the heat into the cave, it surprised him that he found it pleasant.

Siri rummaged through the gifts of the Old Woman. He had not remembered her as generous, so the collection amazed him. There was even salt and a small sack of rice. The water began to simmer, and he threw in a handful of the rice, a bit of the salt, and some of the wild vegetables he had dried—onion, parsley, a potato-like root common to the countryside, herbs he had seen the Old Woman gather, greens of one sort or another, a few of the leeched acorns. He gutted and scaled the fish, ate a bite or two of it raw, and dropped the rest, head and all, into the boiling pot. He had forgotten the smell of cooking food, and saliva gathered at the corners of his mouth as its pungency filled the cave.

All this while, he looked at the girl from time to time. When the smell of the stew and the warmth of the fire did not bring her to life, he drew the cover partly away and began to chafe her hands and arms, her feet and legs. They were well formed like the rest of her, the skin pure and childlike. But he noticed when the quilt slid away that her breasts were not a child's breasts. Methodically he persisted in his efforts to revive her. He was encouraged when the pallor seemed to lessen. After a bit the blue line around her mouth disappeared, and some color crept into lips and cheeks.

Presently she opened her eyes. Before she had time to guard them, Siri saw the flicker of fear behind the blue-green surface. Then it was gone and she regarded him with no expression at all. She made a small move, gathered the cover more closely, then waited, silent, motionless.

As silently, Siri turned away to tend the stew which had boiled down and now made a thick, rich sound as it bubbled over the fire. It was good, he thought, that the Old Woman had sent the pot and the bowl and the cup. And the sharp knife which he had used to gut the fish. The fork and spoon were of no use to him, but the girl might want them. He glanced at her. She continued to watch him with those intense eyes the color of the sea.

It came to him that he was disappointed they were not brown. He had had enough of fair looks in the people of Chelney.

10

The storm marked the beginning of winter. The fury that, overnight, had destroyed the *Laura Ann* was gone by the morning, but snow continued to fall for several days. The muffling silence grew; the cold deepened. The whole land lay muted and subdued. At night, the estuaries began to freeze, and now the fishermen no longer put out from Chelney. Below the cliffs, along the shore, even the sea had lost its voice; the waves crept in among the rocks and scarcely creased the silence of the cave.

That first day, the girl stayed in the nest beneath the blankets. Despite the snow, Siri came and went, securing wood, foraging for food, fishing through the skim of ice on the estuaries. He knew the girl was up and about during his absence, for the wood supply continued to dwindle and the fire itself was warmly bright whenever he returned. But she was in the nest, swaddled in the blankets, when he came in from each wide excursion.

Because of the constant fire, it was necessary to double his efforts to replenish the wood. But he said nothing to break the silence between them. He did not admit to himself that it was pleasant to return to the warmth and the girl. Toward the evening of the fourth day, he came in half frozen, packing a great bundle of wood and two fish. And five eggs that he had managed to filch from an outlying henhouse. He found the girl up and dressed in some of the clothes he had taken from the Old Woman's house. He saw how snugly the spare-cut pants and shirt fitted her sleek roundness. Her pale hair was short as a boy's, but there was no mistaking her body for that of a boy. She withdrew to the other side of the cave. He seemed to give no further thought to her, but set about fixing something they could eat.

Carefully he scraped the scant fat from beneath the skin of one of the fish, dropped this in the pot, cut up some of the wild onion, fried it several minutes in the fat, then broke all five eggs into this, salted them and stirred as he had seen the Old Woman do in times past. The day's efforts had left him ravenous; again he noted how the smell of cooking food made the saliva run in his mouth. Still, he told himself, he would be happy enough with raw fish. He divided the eggs into two portions and set the cup with the girl's share on the floor beside the nest, then returned to the fire and his own meal.

During the day, crouched waiting for a fish to pass beneath the channel that he had broken in the thin ice of the estuary, his buttocks and back had almost frozen. He hated the thought of the confining clothes and wished the silky growth on his body were more like that of the Old Man's, curly and tight as sheep's wool. Still, his own covered him more completely and thus far had allowed him to go in his natural state. But he wondered how he would fare when December's winds began to blow.

Returning to the cave from the estuaries at the end of the day he had stopped near Chelney and stood for some time, staring at the orange-lit windows and the smoke rising straight in the still twilight from the chimneys of the snug houses. A shadow of longing for the early years came, but then he remembered the avid, cruel voices of the hunting men the night he had escaped them with the dying osprey. He turned away and hurried across the frozen land and up the hillside to the cave, forcing the painful memories from his mind.

Now, scarcely thinking of the misery of the day, gratefully he turned his still numb buttocks to the fire's comfort. Yet even after he had finished his food, the chill persisted. Setting his cup aside, he crossed to the back of the cave where he had flung the garments taken from the Old Woman's house. Despite the girl's raid of this meager store, a shirt and pants remained. Siri slipped into these and, fingers fumbling with fastenings grown unfamiliar, he returned to stand before the fire again. The shirt was uncomfortable across the projections of his shoulders and back.

All this while the girl ate slowly with pleasure, her eyes intent on the food, apparently oblivious of him. Still, it pleased him that she liked the supper he had fixed and twice when he looked at her unexpectedly, he thought her eyes slid away from some secret inspection of him. It surprised Siri that he felt a strange quick delight that she took notice of him. But no word passed between them, so after a bit he replenished the fire and, rolled in the blanket, was asleep beside it in moments.

The girl sat for some time watching him, now there was no need to mask her curiosity. After a bit she arose, rinsed the dishes in the cold spring-water, then before settling herself, she crossed and bent above the sleeping boy to study his face once more. She smiled a little, the prominent teeth showing for an instant, the blue-green eyes lighting in the flicker of the flames. He had done her no harm at all and despite the fierceness of his brow and nose she felt no fear of him. Noting he had taken only one blanket for himself, she thrust more sticks into the fire, settled a knotty knurl of oak to back it, returned to the nest and presently was asleep also.

The fire slipped and settled and sprang to new life with its shifting. Perhaps it was this greater heat, perhaps the crackle of the wood that brought the old dreams to haunt Siri once more. Or perhaps the longing that he had smothered in the twilight outside of Chelney came in a twisted form as he lay defenseless. In the black world of his sleep there stood the pyre behind the Meeting House. The villagers with their hard eyes and eager laughter were crowded around it. Several men stepped forward and set torches to the base

147

of the pyre. The nightmare had not dimmed with time. The captive bird struggled to free itself with undiminished desperation; the fire burned as fiercely bright; the flames crept upward as inexorably as before. Strangely, though, the hawk had become half-human, and as it turned to scream at its tormentors Siri saw with horror that it bore his own face.

He twisted in his sleep, thrust with his legs as though to spring away. The blanket, except where it entangled his upper body, was kicked aside in his violence. Thus, presently, the night air cooled his dream and he returned to quiet sleep again.

The loose end of blanket lay close to the fire. After a bit the burning wood shifted and settled once more.

The girl slept heavily in the warmth of the nest. She half roused at some animal sound within the cave. But moments later a hawkish scream split the night, a scream so close, so wild she awoke shaking with terror. She sprang up, crouched, ready to leap away in flight. At the sight of the blanket aflame, and the boy enmeshed and writhing on the stony floor, she bounded from the nest, was beside him with the Old Woman's quilt. As quick as a seal's dive she darted down with it, covered the flames, slicked the quilt along his back. Fresh agony knifed Siri as the pressed fire seared the nerves of his spine. He shrieked again. Even through his own terror he felt the girl tremble. Still, she did not draw away. In seconds the flames were out. Quickly now she took up the knife and cut away the smouldering shirt and pants, then inspected the exposed ruin of skin and singed down that sent its offensive smell throughout the cave. Siri tried not to flinch away.

The girl began to work lightly, gently, flicking off the frizzed growth and bits of charred cloth. She retrieved the egg shells he had cast aside earlier, collected the slick leaving of egg white on her fingertips, spread this on the exposed raw burns. In moments this dried to a thin flexible skin that closed the air from the open wounds. The sharpest agony subsided to a sullen throb. Siri tried to ignore this as he had learned to do with those other pains of body and spirit that had beset him during the past year. Presently, he was almost comfortable.

When he looked at the girl, her eyes, now as green as a morning sea, stared into his. In the firelight, flecks brightened there, bits of mica filtering down to secret deeps. Before he could fathom the obscured expression she looked away.

It had been a long time since anyone had done a personal thing for him; he wondered if she had minded the feel of his back. Did she find him repulsive? He thought perhaps she did. No one except the Old Woman had ever touched or fondled him in any way. And even the Old Woman had cared for him in that fashion only when he was small.

He wanted to say something to the girl, but remembering how harsh his voice had become, he remained silent and she turned away. The nerves of his back, at first numbed with shock, returned to life and began to throb painfully; a chill shook him. Unable to sit still, he wandered restlessly about the cave, glancing now and then at the girl, who had returned to the nest. She plucked at the small sticks along the rim and seemed closed in her own world. Finally he rummaged about in the store of food, found a small unblemished apple, crossed to the nest. With no words he offered the pretty fruit to her, for he could not speak his gratitude. This time when she looked at him her gaze did not slide obliquely away. Instead her lips curved in the slightest of smiles. He saw the smile widen her mouth and relieve the pinched expression of her face. It had been so long since he himself had smiled at another that he had almost forgotten the art. But the hawkish features mellowed, and despite his pain, the dark eyes under their somber brows lightened a little. She took the apple, then touched the nest beside her with one hand. When Siri hesitated, she patted once with the flat of her palm. Finally he settled there.

She bit into the fruit, savored it, before she smiled again, the small tentative smile that sharpened her nose and revealed a bit of the prominent teeth and somehow reminded him more than ever of a seal. The smell of wind and sea and a faint sweet muskiness came to him. In her nearness, he half forgot the throb of his back, and presently, moved by the piquancy of her face, he gave a quick distracted little laugh. Immediately she drew in upon herself, and with averted gaze, ate until the apple was consumed.

Siri's laugh had startled him also, and he too withdrew into his own silence. While she ate, he stared moodily at the fire. The throb increased and the chill shook him despite the blistered heat of the burns. He arose abruptly and left the cave. Outside he stood and stared over the dark sea. The waves were loud against the rocky shore and the wind was beginning to rise.

His deepening chill rattled his teeth. When misery forced him to return to the cave's warmth, he found the girl curled in the nest asleep, the folded quilt laid aside for him. He could tell she was cold beneath her blanket, for she was tucked tightly with only the sharp little nose protruding from the cover.

When he lay down and tried to pull the quilt around himself, it scraped his back and he almost cried out. He managed to lie on his belly and draw the cover over legs and hips. An uneasy sleep finally came, and in it the people of Chelney danced and sang in their dark delight as he stared down at them from his place atop the pyre. Once again they set the torch to the bottom layer of sticks. The wood immediately took the flame. The people's eyes reflected the blaze, and they waited below as eagerly as wolves while the bright tongues of fire licked higher. He gave them no satisfaction until the agony reached his shoulders. In his dream great pinions grew there, and as these began to burn he shrieked aloud. The people laughed and shouted and whirled faster in their dance of frantic glee.

The girl awoke. Her own dreams had been of seas and ships and the avid hungers of sailors below decks. Now she was relieved to find herself in the cave. The embers of the dying fire slipped and settled in the silence. She arose, crossed, thrust in a few more branches, blew them to life. When the warmth and brightness filled the cave, she leaned over the sleeping restless boy. His back had begun to fester. As she inspected it more closely, she could feel the fever of it on her face. He shuddered in every part of his bony frame. She touched his thighs. They were silky beneath her fingers. The memory came of the hard brutal bodies of the sailors, and she smoothed the boy's sides. He seemed so helpless and harried in his sleep that she made little sounds of pity but was unaware that she did this. After a moment she moved back to the nest, rearranged the sticks to widen the center, spread the blanket. Then again beside Siri she urged him up, softly cajoling, and led him across to the new-made couch.

Barely conscious, he muttered in his delirium, but followed the girl meekly enough. When he was settled in the nest, she retrieved the quilt, crept in beside him, covered them both, shielding his back from the chafe of the quilt with her own body. During the long hours of the night she murmured to him whenever he cried out in his terrible dreams. But he no longer shivered and she was comfortable in their shared warmth. Some inner core that she thought had died on the *Laura Ann* stirred, and in the intervals when she did sleep her own night was less haunted.

Next day Siri still floundered in the half-waking dreams. And the next. And by the third morning the girl began to think he might die. But the pile of wood was almost gone and there had been no meat for the pot last night. She knew someone must forage or neither of them would survive. The winter air was as thin and murky as whey when the girl stepped from the cave, and the rising sun was too pale to crease the cold. She stood for a moment, then darted back inside, thrust the last of the sticks into the fire, laid a dense chunk of log atop that, checked to see that the boy was covered. Even as she started to turn away, he thrust the quilt aside, and it was plain he needed to be watched over through this day as she had guarded him during the other restless hours. Still, she had no choice, she must leave him for a while.

Outside once more, the girl moved downhill through the dry powder snow. It was insubstantial and did little to impede her until she reached the lower slopes where it had blown in deep drifts. There, as luck would have it, a rabbit floundered in a hapless attempt to return to its burrow. She had never killed anything before, but with no hesitation she seized a stick, struck the rabbit twice. It gave a small scream at the first blow, died with the second. The girl wept as she picked up the soft body, but she knew at least there would be meat for tonight. Perhaps the rich broth would help the boy survive until his body healed itself. She stopped crying, found a windswept rocky patch, and safely stowed the limp little carcass beneath a small cairn of stones, for there might be other winter hunters afoot, and wood still must be gathered. It surprised her, now, the flare of triumph she felt in having secured the rabbit.

The sun had risen higher and the murky air began to clear as she started downslope once more in her search for wood. It was then she saw the village below. She remembered that glimpse of steady lights from the deck of the dying *Laura Ann*, and gazed now in curiosity. Drawn by a hunger for the company of other people, she continued down the hill, but warily kept from sight. It was possible, she told herself, that the strange boy in the cave was a fugitive from the people clustered together in their safe houses. Otherwise what reason for him to live apart in his spare wild existence?

As the girl watched from the cover of the wooded slope, her sharp hunger for companionship increased. After all, the boy never spoke with her and had laughed only that one time he had studied her face with his fierce eyes. Yet, she remembered, he had saved her life and cared for her while she recovered from her ordeal of the *Laura Ann* and the sea. He had provided food and enough wood to warm the cave day and night.

Beyond that, and her heart opened with gratitude, he had asked nothing of her in return. Now he needed her, so she would not risk betraying him. Later, when he was well or dead, she would try her luck in the village.

She was about to turn away when she noticed a cottage set apart from all the others. An old woman came out of the door and began to fuss with some piece of equipment in the yard; then the woman straightened and turned toward the slope that rose to the dark cliffs. She gazed for so long a time that the girl shifted uneasily, thinking herself discovered. But finally the woman turned wearily about and disappeared within the cottage.

There seemed to be no other movement below and presently the girl set about the task of gathering wood. But she did not forget the old woman and decided when it was time to try her luck with the village that first she would approach the cottage that stood by itself on the outskirts.

11

The rabbit stew was thick and hot and nourishing. But she could persuade Siri to swallow only a sip or two. The dark hours were filled with his nightmares so neither of them truly slept. Next day he worsened. And by the fifth day he lay in a stupor. The girl began to cry each time she looked at him, and at last became convinced the boy was lost to her. Toward dusk she fled the cave.

Fleet and heedless as a wild thing, she leaped down the hill, unaware of the lash of branches or the snag of thorn brush. The thud of her own fist on the door of the cottage revived her senses. A muttered complaint came from within at this sudden racket. It was a man's voice and, frightened, the girl drew back. But when the door swung open a moment later the Old Woman stood there.

The eyes behind their squinted lids were blue-gray chips of granite. They scrutinized the girl, noted the short blond hair springing wildly back from the sharp face, the wide frightened eyes, the lacework of scratches on arms, forehead, cheeks, the snug clothes on the sleek body. Last of all the woman's steady gaze rested on the battered shoes, somehow familiar, and too large for the small feet. The girl standing there in the wintery dusk seemed to her scarcely more than a child. And scantily clad for this season. She sensed that the little thing was poised for instant flight. The Old Man's voice continued to grumble from inside the house. The woman stepped out and pulled the door shut. With the two of them there alone on the stoop, the girl's fright appeared to lessen.

"Yes? What is it?" the Old Woman asked, and her voice was not as unbridled as in other days. The girl was still breathless from the desperate descent, so the woman said almost kindly, "You're not from the village, so what do you call yourself?"

"Thea," the girl said.

"And why did you knock at my door, Thea?"

"Oh, please! You must come and help me!" It was plain that the girl was on the verge of tears.

"Help you with what?" Some impulse made the woman touch the other's shoulder for a moment. Before she could withdraw her hand, the girl who called herself Thea pressed her own palm on top of it as though hungry for contact with another. So they stood thus for a moment until the girl recovered her breath and her voice.

"A boy, up there, in a cave, he's hurt and I'm afraid he'll die. It would be a terrible pity. He's better than any other that I've—" But tears interrupted the words.

The Old Woman's gaze had sharpened and suddenly her hand tightened on the girl's shoulder, shook her. "Stop your crying. How is the boy hurt?"

The severity in the voice made the girl straighten. She drew a little away from the hand, looked into the Old Woman's eyes that bored into her own. Thea managed to say, "He's burned. All along his back and shoulders. He slept close to the fire, and his blanket fell into the flames—" Her voice trembled so much she stopped again.

"Burned," the Old Woman muttered. "That would please Sunderman if he knew." For she had no doubt it was Siri. But then she spoke directly to the girl again. "I must settle my man for the evening. Then I'll come with you. Once Giles is fed he'll drowse by the fire half the night. Can you wait for me there at the edge of the woods? It would be well that no one sees us."

The climb was steep for the Old Woman, who had brought along a large string sack heavy with some mysterious weight. When Thea offered to carry it, the woman gruffly refused though she was forced to stop frequently to rest. Thea, like a small anxious hound, trotted ahead, then back, circled with impatience, made little inarticulate urging sounds. She tried to help by taking the other's arm, but the woman would not or could not hurry. Thea remembered the need for firewood, and to quiet herself gathered branches and pieces of downed trees. Burdened thus, she still outdistanced the woman.

At the cave she was horrified to find Siri lying outside on the flinty stone beneath the night sky. And the fire had died to embers. He was unconscious and cold to her touch. Her anguished cry must have reached the woman, who arrived in a matter of minutes breathing heavily. With no pause she set down the sack, bent to the boy, felt wrist, throat, raised one eyelid with a thumb.

"He still lives," she said, her voice so flat and

hard that Thea was surprised at the pain in those eyes that stared into hers. "Stir up the fire," the woman ordered. "Put on more wood, then set water to heat."

Thea obeyed while the woman lifted Siri as though he were an infant, deposited him in the nest. She arranged the sticks and blankets so she could roll the boy flat on his stomach. In this position and with the fire brightening the cave, it was possible to assess the damage to skin and flesh and those underlying changes that seemed integrated with back, shoulders and upper arms. The festering burns covered these bony ridges. Perhaps it was the heat of the raging fever, but the downy covering of body and legs had become sparse, letting the boy's spare nakedness show through.

Thea heard the woman murmur, "Ah, once my sweet little one. But then truly my Wednesday's child. Now this. Are you indeed a Satan's changeling?"

She began removing various things from the string sack, her rough hands quick with knowledge of a lifetime. First, a pale powder which she mixed with cold water; then clean pads which she soaked in this mixture and laid across the scorched flesh; finally a folded dry cloth to cover it all. After the water had begun to bubble over the fire, the woman cooled a panful with a bit of snow scooped from outside. Then she bathed Siri thoroughly with the warm water and some spicy soap, laving him from head to toe with a firm touch but gently, gently. Next she dried him with care, using a piece of soft towel.

The girl had calmed. Now she sat cross-legged, back to the fire, hands folded in her lap. Her eyes were dark as midnight with only a thin rim of blue around the expanded pupils. Intently they watched every motion of the other's knotty hands. Presently she was aware the Old Woman crooned softly to the boy, a song to soothe the night terrors of a child. After a bit, still humming the lullaby, the woman fished a thin mattresslike pad from her bag of treasures, arranged it on a solid base of springy branches. She motioned to the girl to help her; then deftly the two of them shifted Siri to the soft firm surface. He seemed to rest more easily now, his breath even and not so shallow and quick as before.

Thea touched his cheek and though it still burned, some of the desperate fever had faded. A wave of gratitude for the Old Woman swept her as she stroked the boy's thin face with its hawkish jut of nose. She could not understand her feeling for this one who had never spoken to her and never touched her. When she glanced up, she found the woman watching her.

Confused, the girl looked away. After a moment she said, "What should I call you?"

The woman did not smile, but an ironic amusement lit her eyes. "Emma will do," she said. "Or the villagers call me Old Woman."

"All right. Emma, then." The girl's gaze returned to the boy. "And his name?"

"Siri. Siri Duquesne, if you want the whole of it."

"Siri." Thea tried the name. "Siri." She smiled. The woman was surprised at the way the sharp little face softened and changed with the smile. The girl asked, "Siri Duquesne? And you? Emma Duquesne?"

"Yes."

"Siri's grandmother?"

"Mother."

"Oh," the girl said, and colored along her rounded high cheekbones.

They both fell silent. Presently Thea settled with her back to the fire again. Twice, Emma Duquesne changed the cool soaked pads on Siri's back. At last she covered him closely, but then continued to fuss with the things she had brought.

Finally she said, "The pads should be kept cool and moist for the first day. Do not let them dry or they will stick to the sores. Soon the oozing will stop, then a sprinkle of powder from this small jar and the dry cloth will suffice. He should do now until morning." But she did not leave immediately and returned to the arrangement of her supplies from the string bag.

Exhausted from the past sleepless days and nights, Thea drowsed. Later she was dimly aware of being led to the nest, settled on something soft that lay over the resilient base, and covered warmly. For a moment she felt the brightening of the fire as it was stoked to last the night, then dreamless sleep took her, and she did not know when the woman departed.

Emma Duquesne returned the next day, and the next. But as Siri improved and became conscious of her presence, she withdrew. She told Thea that the Old Man needed her. She said he had fallen into a spell of illness when his boat was destroyed last summer, and now became ugly and quarrelsome when she was gone for long. She inspected Siri's back once more. It no longer festered and was beginning to heal properly. His fever was gone entirely. Thea saw that he tried to find words to say to the Old Woman, but none came. Emma and Siri Duquesne looked dumbly at each other, then the woman left and did not return.

Thea was sorry for this and missed her, but soon, with Siri enough improved to accompany her for short distances from the cave, life changed. By this time, Thea had become almost as able as Siri in the arduous work of ice fishing and snaring game and digging roots. Together, as he regained his strength, they secured their livelihood and found joy in each other and in their growing closeness.

Though Thea delighted in her own animated talk to Siri each evening when they had returned to the cave, she accepted his silence with no question. Yet one day when they searched for game in the thickets near the swamp, they became separated. At first he searched for her calmly enough, but when he could not find her, a terrible panic seized him. Frantically he beat through the tangle of old vines and bushes, and at last her name thrust up from his belly, past the frozen organ of his voice, to burst forth upon the winter air, painful, hot, loud, harsh.

"Thea! Where are you! Thea! Thea!"

She heard the great cry and the fear behind it and came running. She threw her arms around him to give comfort.

Helplessly he whispered against her neck. "I— I thought you were lost in the swamp."

"Dear Siri," she laughed, fondling his head. "I

was certain you could say no words, yet you shouted my name so loudly it almost stopped my heart!"

But she was crying too, for no one had ever called her thus or cared if she was lost or not.

In the cave that night they lay in love together for the first time. It was a wonder to them both. He had thought that only flying could bring such soaring joy. She had never dreamed that this act which life had taught her to fear could be a loving, gentle thing.

Now, as the days passed, on occasion they sat in close conversation. But usually, wandering the wide wintery world, they were silent together, and because of this, they moved freely over the land, as at home as two wild creatures. Then it seemed only a smile and a touch was needed between them; and their love in the long nights.

They always avoided the village, so, the people of Chelney knew nothing of them.

The weeks flew by and winter began to loosen its tight grip on the land. For the first time in all her years Thea found herself happy and almost content. Yet one day when Siri came upon her alone on the high slope near the cave, he became uneasy, for he saw how intently she gazed at the cottages far below and at the small figures of people moving about the yards and along the Chelney road. Watching, his uneasiness grew. The girl's face was as sharp as a hungry seal's, her lips a little open and drawn back to show the tips of her teeth. When she felt him standing there above her, she turned, then suddenly smiled, reached her hand toward him. His uneasiness gone, laughing, he swooped down to sit beside her, took her hand and loved the feel of her fingers entwined with his. He put an arm about her and willingly she settled against him. There was the fresh sea smell of her and the sweet muskiness. And they both forgot about Chelney.

Spring was late. The storms had early lost their fury but came quietly, at intervals, so the ice remained until the end of April and the fishermen of Chelney did not begin their work in earnest until the first part of May. This year there were fewer hands than ever to do the work. The best of the boys, as they came of an age to be truly useful, continued to filter away from the village in increasing numbers. These did not return. And one by one the more enterprising girls followed.

No new Leader had been chosen this year; Bartel Sunderman refused to relinquish the post and no one was anxious to cross him. They all remembered it was he who had seen the danger of Siri and the ospreys and driven them away. The village owed him something for that. Besides, Sunderman let it be known that whoever was against him was on the side of Satan. What had become of Siri Duquesne none knew. And none cared.

The Old Woman said nothing. She had little to do with the villagers now. Since Giles Duquesne no longer contributed to the general good of Chelney, he seemed forgotten by the others. No one bothered to visit the old pair. After all, each family had its own concerns. The Old Woman sorrowed as she saw her man fading and slowly dying. In her heart she felt it was her own fault. The boat she had burned had been his life. Without his work he was nothing, and he was too proud to sign on with another even if he had been asked.

But the boy and girl knew nothing of the difficulties in Chelney. They lived their life apart, each day finding new joy in each other. It was the first time that either had lived in the full circle of love, caring for, cared for, giving and receiving.

The fever had burned away the down that covered Siri's body, so to protect himself from the cold he began to wear the clothes that the Old Woman had brought one day before she had ceased to come. The pinion-like ridges involving his shoulders and back gradually became less noticeable as a pleasing layer of firm flesh began to pad his angular frame. And Thea prospered also. Her eyes were clear and bright, her skin glowed, her hair grew longer and became thick and glossy. She sang softly to herself for no reason at all. Only from time to time when she stood brooding over the sight of Chelney, did unrest cloud her apparent joy.

As chilly April drew to a close, Siri watched the skies for the return of the migrant flocks. He did not have quite the avid passion for them as of other years. Still, he felt certain the birds would excite Thea, so he continued his vigil with anticipation. He promised himself he would take her to the estuaries to watch the geese. These birds, with their gregarious ways and busyness and bustle, were like feathered villagers. Thea would surely delight in them. Perhaps then she would find no need to watch from the hill to see what transpired in Chelney. It made him increasingly uneasy that she still did this in any idle moment. She took particular interest in the set-apart cottage, and one day told Siri that during his illness she had become fond of Emma Duquesne, who seemed to Thea kind beneath the rough surface.

"I'd like to visit her," she said. Siri turned away and went down to hunt alone among the estuaries.

Each day he continued to watch the skies. One afternoon he said, half to himself, "I wonder if my osprey will return."

"Osprey?" Thea asked.

"Some call them sea hawks or fish hawks."

"Ah! Yes. The hawk that dives for fish." She smiled up at him from where she sat. "Tell me about your osprey." She leaned back, braced by her arms, so her hair blew free in the freshening breeze that today carried the smell of spring.

He loved the way she looked, there on the rocks above the reach of the waves, and it warmed him when the smile lit her lively eyes and eased the sharpness of her face. He settled beside her and, as always now, took her hand. She put one arm around his shoulders and leaned against him so he felt her warmth and her small firm breast where it pressed his arm.

"Tell me about your osprey," she urged.

"I'd rather hold you." He laughed and kissed her.

Nevertheless he told her of all the birds and most particularly of the ospreys. And also of his last season among the estuaries and his hazardous climb on the cliffs. It pleased him that she held tightly to him at the thought of this latter danger. He said nothing of his difficulties with the people of Chelney. And presently they were laughing

170

again, then off to find something for the stewpot, as their vigorous outdoor existence left them forever hungry. And there was that other sweet hunger, quieted in the long nights together in the nest. Then their loneliness was a forgotten thing.

Because of the late cold it was the end of the first week in May when the earliest flocks came in, and on the same day, Chelney's fishermen returned to their long hours of boats and nets and toil.

Truly Thea did take great delight in the spectacle of all the circling, calling, excited, noisy birds. Siri showed her how each kind attracted its mate and where they built their nests. He could tell her which bird had run across this wet sandy stretch or that by the prints left behind. Or when the two of them chanced on some nest, deserted or left unattended for a moment, he knew which bird had laid the eggs there by the color and marking, size and shape. He was able to mimic the separate calls that echoed through the spring skies and to name the possessor of each of those sweet or shrill or raucous sounds.

He had been right about the geese too. Thea was entranced by the great buffy Canadas with their glossy black heads and white chin patches. Siri told her how these largest of the geese mated faithfully for life, traveling the tremendous migratory flyways side by side, nesting together, and raising their young, until one died of storm or old age or some hunter's gun, leaving the other bereft and solitary.

When he saw she grew sad at the thought of the tragedy that must surely overtake each pair, he said that there were many more birds who had only one season together; these fickle lovers found other mates with each new season.

"—with no past and no future to blight their lives," he said, expecting her to smile.

But she said, her eyes somber, "And no joy of memories, or time laid on time with one another so life has some meaning."

He laughed half derisively and declared she spoke of people, not birds, and refused to say he thought her right even when she withdrew and would not respond to him for half a day. But this spat was quickly forgotten.

Increasingly, they found themselves content only if they were with each other. Thus he was dismayed when she asked him one day, "Don't you ever miss Chelney? Will you never return there?"

He felt her study him with those blue-green eyes, so like the sea, but he did not look at her.

Instead he gazed at the pebbles beneath his feet. They were shining and full of color from the quiet waves. He chose a red one, as dark as venous blood, and turned it in his fingers.

"Why should I miss Chelney?" he finally said. "There's no reason to go back there."

"It's your home."

He laughed, swept an arm at cliffs and sea and sky. "This is home." And he skipped the red stone across the water.

"Your mother and father live in Chelney."

"I'm nothing to them, nor they to me."

"Yet she came when she thought you were dying."

Siri stared at her, his fierce eyes darkening. Then with no other word he rose and walked away from her, off down the hill. Thea's voice followed him.

"Well, *I* am lonely. I should like to visit with Emma Duquesne!"

Now she arose also and without him climbed the hill toward the cave. She turned about at the top and scanned the hillside and flats below. After some time she saw him. He walked at the fringe of the marshes, on past Chelney. Distance swallowed his solitary figure when he reached the estuaries.

Though she was asleep when he returned toward morning, she smiled when he touched her and took his hand in hers, and banished his coolness with her own warmth.

12

Oren Sunderman sat in the bow of the seiner. Covetously, his eye roamed the length of the craft. He was the eldest son, and some day this would be his. For a moment he turned to watch his father, who labored at the heavy nets. Such strenuous effort might shorten a man's life.

Oren was seventeen. This year Bartel had taken him on as apprentice seaman and assigned him duties that gave him authority over the other two boys of the crew, and even over several of the men. He spread himself in this role and was disliked by them all. This mattered little to Oren. He had seen, in his father, that the important thing in life was to gain power over others. He thought of how he would run the fleet and the village when his father was gone. Then all the girls of Chelney would be eager for his favor and he could sift and winnow among them to find the one that pleased him most. This thought brought pictures to mind that made him smile as he lolled against the lee rail watching the boil of the sea along the vessel's bow.

"Oren!" Bartel Sunderman roared.

The young man swung his bulky body about and ambled back to take his place beside his father at the nets. He strained and seemed to exert great strength; in reality he let the burden fall upon the man.

"The boat will be mine," Oren thought. "Perhaps even the leadership of Chelney. And, of course, the girls. I can cast them all aside, except several of the best. Then it will take some time to make the final choice—"

"Blast you!" grated Bartel. "Lean your shoulder into it, Oren! You're a lazy beast."

So the son postponed his dream for another time.

The villagers were pious, thus the men did not fish on Sundays. It was almost twilight on a lazy

Sabbath early in June that Oren, by fate or luck, saw the strange girl at the door of the Old Woman's cottage. He had gone out in search of some sport to enliven the evening. But there were scarcely any young people his own age left in the village—only a few girls whose mothers kept them close on Sundays. And Oren was tired now of harrying the smaller children. Idly he moved his burly bulk along the road that led off south of the village. His pale eyes with their pale lashes wandered over the empty scene. Unless hunting, he cared nothing for the birds and beasts, and he was unaware of the wild beauty of the Chelney coast.

His heavy-jawed face became intent when he noticed the girl running toward him along the road. Because of the poor light at this hour, he was unable to see her clearly. She appeared fey and small. Certainly unlike any girl he had known before. She did not belong in Chelney. As she came flying along the deserted road, he saw that she was entirely alone. Oren smiled. But then, to his disappointment, the girl turned in at the path of the Old Woman's cottage. He watched as she knocked at the door, which presently was opened by the Old Woman. He could not hear what passed between the two, but after a moment the girl entered. The door closed behind her.

Though Oren waited until well after dark, the girl did not come out again. He promised himself to watch for her, and cursed the fact he had to work aboard the boat tomorrow.

It was not until the next Sunday that he saw her again. She was with the Old Woman, who, that day, made one of her rare trips into the village to do a frugal shopping at the general store that served housewife, fisherman, handyman, and child. All the goods, laid out in tempting array, had been brought by the supply ship, the *Sea Horse.* As a convenience for the men of the village who worked six days of the week, the proprietor of the store was allowed to do business for a few hours each Sunday after church. He stocked everything from rice to fineries, from fishhooks and nets and line to nails and bolts and penny sweets.

Thea walked close beside Emma Duquesne. This was her first trip into Chelney, and though she had been hungry for the company of others, now she looked half anxiously about. When she thought of Siri, her stomach hurt; she wished herself in the cave with him close beside her. They had quarreled though, and the last she had seen of him he was scrambling up the hillside toward the top of those awesome cliffs.

He had flung the words down at her. "Go stay with the Old Woman if that's what you want! I'll live with the sea hawks! At least *their* fierceness is a natural thing. They're not so cruel as those hawks that live in Chelney!"

She tried to tell him she only wished to visit with Emma Duquesne for a few days. But he turned and flew up the rough way before she could speak, and she was afraid to follow. The thought of Siri's stubborn spirit had made her so angry that she whirled away and dashed off down the hillside. His words had dismissed her as though he no longer cared. All her old doubts sprang to life as she ran; she promised herself she would not return until he came and asked her to.

Finally, below, she made her way across the flats and then to the woman's cottage. A man had been coming toward her from the direction of the village, a young man, thick of body, but she scarcely noticed him; her only thought was how to persuade Emma to take her in, at least for a few days. She did not intend to stay for long. Surely Siri would come back to the cave. Yes, she was certain of that. And when his anger cooled, he would find her and ask her to return to him.

Then came the doubt of how the Old Woman would receive her. But that worry proved unnecessary. When she told Emma that she had come to visit for a few days, the woman's look of gratitude was almost hidden. But Thea, sensitive to small signs that showed another's secret heart, knew that Emma was glad for her visit. In the cottage she saw how bleak life was for the Old Woman. Giles Duquesne lay flat in bed. There was none of the man left who had once captained his own vessel. Now he stared unseeing at the rafters; his breath rasped, coarse and uneven; his limbs shook with a constant tremor.

"He had a spell of fainting at the first of the month," the Old Woman said. "It was all I could do to lift him into bed." Little emotion showed in her voice, but Thea saw the desolation in the flinty eyes. "Nothing lives but his body, and that scarcely does." She pulled the blanket a little higher on the sagging white chest. Giles only stared at the ceiling beams.

Emma asked a few questions about Siri, but when she learned he had fully recovered from the burns, she lost interest and did not mention him again. In her loneliness, she welcomed Thea and her soft ways, and began to treat her as she would have a daughter if fate had given her one.

So now, as they entered Chelney, and the girl drew close to Emma, they linked arms and walked along as though they truly belonged together. It was then that Oren saw the girl for that second time. He watched her from a distance, noting the way she moved and the sleekness of her neat buttocks beneath the snug trousers, and the way the shirt pulled across her breasts. He changed direction, angled over, and sidled up to the two as they walked along.

"You're new to Chelney." He tried to make his voice friendly as he looked down at the girl. "I could show you around."

Thea glanced at him, then looked away. It was the Old Woman who answered. "Aye. New. But not that new."

Oren kept pace with them. Some of the friendliness was gone when, still ignoring the Old Woman, he persisted. "Where are you from? No boat that I know of has put in at Chelney with passengers."

He looked the girl over from head to foot and back again. He was certain she flushed from pleasure at his attention, or from eagerness at what might happen between them if only the Old Woman were not about. In reality, it was anger and fright that had raised Thea's color. She had seen those appraising looks in other men's eyes.

Emma Duquesne stopped and faced Oren. She had disliked him as a child and had no use for him as a man. "Go on about your business, Oren Sunderman, if you have any business to go about."

At this, Oren turned openly ugly. "My father

wants to know about any stranger in the village, Old Woman. Where did this one come from?" He still watched the girl, and now in an attempt to ingratiate himself with her he smirked a little, tried to soften his voice. "We're choosy about who lives in Chelney."

"Not choosy enough!" Emma's laugh was harsh as her hard eyes swept him. "Tell your father she's a niece of mine from downcoast. Now leave us alone or I'll shout from the Meeting House steps what all the girls whisper about you, Oren. It's nothing you'd want Bartel to hear."

Though Emma Duquesne had not the slightest idea of what the girls might whisper, Oren must have had some guilty twinge, for the threat succeeded. The Old Woman smiled in triumph as Bartel's boy dropped behind them, then turned away to find some other amusement.

But Oren promised himself that if Emma Duquesne's niece stayed in Chelney he would, somehow, manage to know her.

The first night of their separation, Siri returned to the cave. He assured himself that Thea would creep silently into the nest beside him before morning. He awoke a dozen times in the night and reached for her. It was almost dawn when he could bear the empty cave no longer.

182

In the darkness he scrambled up the steep way to the high plateau. As though some black fear dogged his heels, he rushed and stumbled. At the top, more calmly, he made his way to the cliff's rim and settled there. The morning lamps of Chelney came on one by one. His hawk's vision had diminished. Perhaps that recent raging fever had dimmed it. Or was it only that such acute sharpness of eye was no longer needed in the easier life of the last months?

Yet on this morning, he could still distinguish the set-apart light of the Old Woman's place. He tried to imagine Thea there. He pictured her, even now, asleep in his boyhood bed. He smiled a little, remembering she had never liked to stir from the nest in those early hours that he loved most of all the day. Alone in that little room now, did she miss the feel of him beside her? There was a chill along his cheeks in the dawn breeze; he was glad he smiled or he might have thought he was crying.

After the first days of Thea's absence, he conquered the feel in his own body that half of him was gone, and by the end of June he had trained himself not to return to the cave with foolish hope. His mind responded well; his heart was more difficult to subdue. Though he told it that love was always an uncertain thing, it remained stubborn and long retained the imprint of tender looks, musky odors, murmur of voice, touch of hand, warmth of body against body. These memories almost destroyed him; and, though he wandered the estuaries, he saw and heard nothing of the sweet stir of early summer. Wary instinct still kept him safe from any eyes in Chelney, as each day he threaded the edge of the marshes on his way to the most northerly deserted tideflats.

It was here, at the end of June, that a flicker of last year's excitement sprang to life within him. He had trudged miles of the flat-washed shore and barren sand bars. As the afternoon waned, he turned back to the south, for he had taken to sleeping on the harsh plateau above the cliffs. Near the marsh, as he approached a stand of old trees now half drowned by some change in tidal channels and jagged with upthrust dead snags, a shadow swept across him. Memory halted his step. He glanced up. There above was a familiar slant of wings. An osprey circled, came steeply down with a fish clutched in its talons. The hawk came to rest on the edge of a great disordered pile of sticks arranged in the crown of the highest dead snag. A female awaited him there. Siri knew she would still be protecting half-grown fledglings.

This male was smaller than the old one of last

year, the nest not so huge as one established seasons ago. Was this sea hawk one of the offspring that last summer had departed the nest on the cliffs? Unlikely. That male should not mate until its third year. Late in the afternoon, Siri ended his vigil. As he made his way along the marshes, past Chelney and up the hillside toward the steep bluffs, his spirit began to reawaken.

Yet before he went on up to the plateau, something moved him to see the cave again. He found it still empty. It depressed him that he had not given up hope entirely. Restless, he moved through the dim interior. The last of the light scarcely reached here. Thea's presence continued to haunt the place. It seemed her sea-fresh scent lingered. The quickening that had begun within him today as he watched the ospreys now was gone. Desperately he flung out of the cave. For a breath of time he thought there was a movement across the darkening hillside. With a last quick hope he called her name. Only silence answered. He charged up the steep way to the cliff tops. The effort purged his mind of its darkness and he let his thoughts return to the ospreys. Slowly his spirit revived.

That night he slept soundly. It was the first time since Thea left that his longing for her did not awaken him. Next day he set about exploring the cliffs. And the next. He risked himself with climbs to impossible ledges. He lay for hours scanning the wide sky, scarcely letting himself imagine that the old osprey also might have returned this year. Methodically he searched the nearer cliffs, then each day moved farther to the south. At the end of the week he had decided that the only ospreys on Chelney's coast were the new pair nesting in the farthest estuary. Still, there was one final rise of cliff that he was determined to explore.

Siri had never been so far from Chelney. He discovered that this out-thrust escarpment was the headland between the rugged coast he knew and the softer hills and downs that could be seen far off toward the south. The wind was more fierce here than on last year's ledges, the cliffs more sheer with no narrow rocky beach; thus the waves washed the lower reaches where the cliffs plunged directly into the sea. He had almost fallen half a dozen times in descents to inadequate shelves. Even eagles did not nest on these bleak faces. It was on the last day he had allotted himself to search here, and when he had almost given up hope, that he found the old osprey.

This day's descent had brought him by a hazardous route farther down the precipice than he had been before. From the narrow shelf he stood upon, he saw another, lower still. On its inadequate space was the great pile of sticks and debris that marked a hawk's nest. There a young female osprey brooded her chicks. Siri's heart rocked him with its fast light flutter. When he moved for a better view, the female saw him. She screamed several times, rose from the nest in a short disturbed flight, settled again, watched him with fixed golden gaze. He squatted there motionless. After a while she forgot him.

It seemed an eternity passed before the male appeared, flying in from the south with its catch grasped in the great horny talons. The hawk alighted, dropped the fish within the nest. This male seemed as large as the young female. An old bird, Siri decided. He began to hope. He moved again and called to the male. At Siri's cry, the bird wheeled away, rose high in one mighty thrust of wings, then with an angry scream flew down and in at the intruder on the upper ledge.

As the hawk plunged with a great buffeting of wings, Siri echoed the bird's scream with his own. The old osprey changed direction with a noisy flurry of pinions, came to rest on the far end of the ledge. Intently it eyed the stranger. Siri spoke softly, churred in the way he remembered. At last the hawk ruffled all the feathers of its neck and body, then drew them tight again. It sat for a long while, gazing with unblinking golden eyes. With no other sign, it finally flew off and returned to its hunting. When it reappeared with another catch it no longer seemed to notice Siri, who smiled to himself, his dark eyes lighting with the old fierce wild joy.

That night he dreamed of flying with the hawks. And he no longer reached out for Thea in the dark hours.

By the middle of July, with the days hot and the nights gentle, he shed the confining clothes. During this time he had dared to visit the cave a time or two. Now he went there no more. Naked, he found that his gaunt frame was already sprouting the protective down. It seemed to thicken with each passing day until he had the glossy sheen of last season. With Thea gone, and the comfort of the cave and ample food a thing of the past, he had lost the pleasing layer of flesh. The rack of his bones became increasingly light, more airy. His ribs pushed forward. The thinness of arms and shanks made feet and hands seem larger than before.

These alterations in his body accelerated, outstripping those of last season. His spirit no longer resisted the changes that had disturbed him a year ago. What did it matter now if he was unlike other men? Along his shoulders and back and upper arms where the charred flesh had once caused such agony, the ridges became more pronounced day by day. He was certain the projections there were greater than those before the disaster of the fire.

And his heart and mind changed. There came the certainty that Thea was gone from his life. Soon, he promised himself, he would forget her entirely.

13

All through the spring the seiners had been busy, each hold jammed with its silvery catch at day's end. Even by the last of June this good fortune had not abated. Nevertheless, dark talk spread through Chelney; it was all in secret, so Bartel Sunderman had no way of knowing how the rumors ran. The whispers were that Chelney itself was dying. What family had not lost son or daughter, or both, to the outside world? Since early times, there had always been a wild one or two each season who preferred to try his fortune elsewhere. But last spring and summer and fall, a dozen young people had departed, and this year the exodus had accelerated.

"To lose our children!" one wife lamented. "A curse blacker than last season's when the fish disappeared from the sea."

"Sunderman rid Chelney of that first evil and the fish returned. Since then, our men have had nothing but good fortune," another reminded her.

But a third woman, angry and frightened, cried, "So why does Sunderman do nothing now to save our young people for us?"

The first laughed bitterly. "He still has his Oren. The woes of the rest of us mean nothing to him. Last year our curse was Siri and the hawks. I'm beginning to think that this year our curse is Sunderman himself."

An idle sour jest, but the women happened to repeat it to their men, and they to others, until soon the poisonous whispers ran through Chelney.

But the Duquesne cottage was separated from the village with its problems. Thea had enjoyed Emma's company for the first few days and kept her longing for Siri to herself. She seemed happy and smiled often as the two women, old and young, chatted endlessly together. Dim memory recalled to the Old Woman her own girlhood and her own mother. There had been much talking then too. But she had married early, and Giles Duquesne, even in his youth, had been a silent one. This year he had become useless for everything. Yet the burden of the Old Man, now it was shared, did not weigh so heavily; and under Thea's spritely influence, some of the Old Woman's vitality revived.

Thea and Emma began to go into the village each day. Everyone accepted the girl as one of the Duquesne family and asked few questions, for their usual curiosity was stifled by their own worries over Chelney's fate. So Thea found pleasure in Emma's company, or in chatting with the village women, or occasionally fondling or playing with the village children. Yet the thought of Siri haunted any idle moment. One night she started up from a dream of him. For an instant she was ready to spring from bed and run to the cave to see if all was well. And beyond that, to hold him in her arms, to feel his warmth and angularity against her own softness, to be together in the old loving way. Yet there was the promise she had made herself not to return until he asked her. When she remembered the Old Woman's burdens and the need for her here, she settled in bed again. But sleep did not come for a long while, for Siri continued to haunt her mind.

The need for him grew each day and by the end of the third week Thea could stand it no longer. "Tomorrow I'll be leaving," she told Emma. "Already I've stayed too long."

In truth, she suddenly felt wicked for leaving Siri alone for such a time with no effort from her to reconcile them. Yet she had hoped, each day, that he would come to her. Was he angry still, had he forgotten her? Hope flickered that perhaps he burned to see her with the same longing that seized her in the night. She had no doubt that he had returned to the cave.

But Emma Duquesne said, "Ah, not tomorrow! That is Sunday. I have a bonnet for you, and a dress I stitched as a surprise. Could we not go to church, the two of us together?" She watched Thea, certain the girl would not resist her.

"I *must* leave." The sharp face was pinched, the eyes dark as a sunless sea. "Siri will think I've forgotten him—"

"Oh, Siri it is?" Emma's tone was acid, but then she managed a smile. She saw the girl as pliable, easy to control, and though the woman had no intent to injure Siri, her first concern was to guard her own welfare.

"What will I do without you?" She wiped at her eyes with her apron. "You have brightened my days and eased my heart. Even the Old Man seems less of a burden with you here."

She saw that Thea was touched by her difficulty, and beyond that, the girl was gratified because someone needed her. What the woman did not see was Thea's longing to be with Siri again. The years had made her forget those urgent passions. So, Emma pressed her advantage.

"At least stay until after we go to church tomorrow," she said. "Or the dress I sewed will be for naught. It would please me so for everyone to see you in it, and us sitting side by side like mother and daughter."

Thea hesitated a moment, then pressed the other's hand. But despite her smile, the fine flesh of the girl's face seemed taut, the high cheekbones sharp against the skin.

"All right," she finally said. "We shall go to church in the morning. There will be plenty of time for me to reach the cave before dark."

Emma only nodded and smiled. And thought of ways she could detain the girl longer, for she continued to forget the needs of youth and to misread the sweet temper as weakness.

So after all, fate or fortune can rule a life. If Thea had not waited for Sunday to return to the cave and to Siri, then Oren would have been at sea on the little seiner that would one day be his. And perhaps the people of Chelney, in the end, would have solved their problem in other ways.

Thea arranged her day with care. She was truly fond of the Old Woman and wished to escape with no argument or hard feeling between them. Perhaps someday when things were easy with her and Siri, she could come here again for a short visit.

"But never for so long as this has been," she promised herself, and pressed her hands against her body to quiet the painful excitement there. Soon she would be with Siri again. Her eagerness for him obsessed her.

The church service dragged interminably. Someone snored softly behind her, a fly crawled undisturbed across a bald pate in the second row, dust motes hung golden in sunlight slanting down from a loft window. And Emma watched her all the while.

Finally Thea glanced up, smiled, leaned to whisper in the woman's ear, "It's truly a lovely dress."

She ran her hands along the cloth as if to smooth it, though in reality she had first pressed them there to quiet the secret longing, painful but pleasurable now that she knew it would soon end. Her face was flushed, and she hoped the Old Woman read this as delight with the new clothes.

Thea's gaze shifted again to her own lap, studied the fine material with its tiny sprigs of blue and green flowers. The background was white, but not quite white. Thea guessed the Old Woman had had the cloth for a long time. She warmed at the thought that Emma Duquesne cared enough for her to make not only the dress and bonnet, but also to bring out the pair of black slippers, old and dainty. These were far too small for the Old Woman's feet as they had become, but, even so, a little large for Thea.

Emma beamed and secretly glanced about to see if the two of them were duly noticed. She with a sweet daughter, a picture she had long treasured in fantasy. The monotonous service did not engage her; instead her thoughts returned to the early morning when Thea had spoken in gratitude for the welcome given her at the Duquesne cottage.

"The child was preparing the way to leave easily this afternoon," the Old Woman decided. "I'll persuade her to stay another day or two. Perhaps even a week." She smiled, sure of her own powers, and even began to plan some permanent arrangement.

A cave is no place for the girl to live. And Siri surely, is no proper— But here the Old Woman's mind shied away and busied itself with other things.

After church, Emma lingered to spread herself a little before the other women. When she turned to go, Thea was nowhere in sight. Half angry, the woman returned alone to the cottage. There she found the dress, the bonnet, the little shoes neatly laid out on the well-made bed. Beside them was a note. It was carefully written, but the Old Woman had done little reading in her lifetime and it took her a long while to decipher the words.

Emma, I cannot bear to say good-bye to you. I would surely cry. That is why I said my thanks earlier. You must know how much I loved it here. It was so good to have another woman to talk with. When Siri and I have things settled with each other, I'll come and see you again. Maybe we will both come. Until then, please think of me with love, as I shall think of you.

Thea

While Emma Duquesne struggled with this, Thea herself had begun the climb up the lower slopes below the cliffs. In her excitement to reach the cave, she had not once glanced back along the road from Chelney. She did not know that she was followed.

Oren Sunderman had seen her slip away from the gathering outside the church and trailed her to the cottage. When she disappeared within, he thought of trying to enter also, but then he remembered the Old Man, and instead hid beside the road. Presently Thea reappeared, this time dressed in the old snug pants and worn shirt. Oren smiled when she struck off, away from Chelney, toward the empty land to the south. At a discreet distance he followed. He thought how secretly gratified she would be to see him when they were completely alone. He was puzzled, though, at how purposefully she hurried along.

Thea pressed rapidly ahead even after she began the climb. The slopes became increasingly steep, and she was winded by the time she sighted the dark opening of the cave. Village living had made her soft. She was torn between excitement and uneasiness. On the hillside below, there had been the sense of someone behind her, a slip of rock, a crackle of brush too sharp in the light breeze, a glimpse of movement, seen sidelong, but gone by the time she had turned her head.

"Foolishness," she told herself. "Who would follow me from Chelney!" And her thoughts returned to Siri.

The excitement started again when she pictured him awaiting her within the cave. Eagerly she called his name aloud, rushed up the last steep rise, burst into the dim cool shelter. The cave was empty.

She blinked away the tears and chided herself. "Do you think he has been sitting here for three weeks with nothing to do but wait for you?"

And she thought of all the work that was necessary to keep body and spirit together in the wild existence. Soon he would return. With assurance, she settled to wait. Time dragged and after a bit the deserted, unused air about the place made her restless. Yet, she forced herself to lie down in the nest, close her eyes, and try to sleep.

"Let him find me here," she whispered, suppressing all her doubts. "He will come and hold me and kiss me. And all will be as before between us."

She awoke with a start. The light at the entrance had waned. The day was almost gone. The excitement had left her body. She moved heavily to the opening, stared at the late sky and the quiet sea.

"Is he still angry?" she murmured. "Or has he forgotten me?" And blamed herself for ever leaving to visit the Old Woman.

Already her mind was busy with thoughts of what she must do to sustain herself here, for she was determined to wait, and hope for Siri's return. The cave was empty of food, so now she must manage something for dinner. With little spirit she moved out along the hillside. Then her heart leaped with joy. A movement in the shadows there. She could think of no one but the wild fierce boy who was like no other she had ever known.

"Siri! Siri!" she cried and rushed toward the half-hidden figure that even as she ran came out to meet her.

Oren Sunderman laughed. "What do you know of Siri? He's dead. Or at least he's gone from Chelney forever."

"*No, no,*" was all the girl said, which made no sense at all to Oren. Her appearance there had startled him. Earlier she had outdistanced him, and disappeared by the time he reached the steeper bluffs. Like the other villagers he had always shunned this bleak land. But today, rather than return unfulfilled to Chelney, he had followed the girl. When he lost sight of her on the rough slopes he was certain she had continued on to the top. With some trepidation he decided to wait until she descended. There was no way she could escape him, for there was only this one route to return to Chelney. To the right, thickets and thorny brush blocked the way, and off to the left there were only the sheer faces of the cliffs and the rocky shore. Through timidity he did not explore in either direction.

The fact was that superstitious fear about this cliffy region filled Oren, and it was with great uneasiness he managed to wait. Yet the thought of the way the girl had looked in the dainty dress, and later in the pants that fit her like skin, had kept him there. Now, with the afternoon almost gone, he finally arose from the thicket where he crouched. He had no appetite for staying here until dark.

The sight of Chelney below reassured him somewhat. He squinted in the late light, studying the town, looking for some familiar form moving about the streets or the outlying countryside. Oren was poor company for himself and the silence made him nervous. Presently he did see a figure off at the fringe of the marshes. It stayed partially screened by the tangled growth there. Once past the area of Chelney, though, whoever it was seemed to become more bold, moving out across the flat land in this general direction. Before he could wonder further about the furtive form, Oren heard a sudden sound behind him. He swung about. Thea ran lightly toward him.

It struck him as ridiculous that she called for Siri. It was this that made him laugh. Had the Old

Woman been feeding lies about her blighted son to the girl? When he saw her eyes widen with fear of him, he was pleased. He knew that girls, for decorum's sake, always feigned modesty and fright. Yet, when he reached for her she eluded him. Excited by the prospect of the chase, he lunged again. He had not time to ward off the unexpected blow. Thea put all of her slight weight behind the heel of her hand as it plunged against Oren's nose. He squealed with agony. Tears blinded him. By the time his sight had cleared, Thea was far down the hill, bounding off toward Chelney. She ran like a hound-harried rabbit. In Chelney the Old Woman would protect her.

Despite his fear that night might overtake him here, Oren sank to the ground and nursed his throbbing nose. He had heard the bone crack, now he wondered how badly it was broken.

Siri had spent this day at the farthest estuary, where he had discovered the young male osprey and its mate in the drowned tree snag. His spirits lifted as he made his way south, late in the afternoon, toward the high plateau for a safe night's rest. His mind was filled with the thought of the hawks, and with the possibility that the old one might have returned to the cliffs. Yet as he neared the vicinity of the cave, his yearning for Thea drew him in that direction. If she had not filled his whole mind, he might have discovered Oren huddled in the brush.

For moments after Siri passed, Oren was afraid to move. It was one thing to torment the outcast boy who used to run through the village while the other children shouted in glee, another to face, alone, this fierce wild thing who was boy no longer. Thinking himself safe at last, Oren started to arise. Quickly he shrank down again, for Siri had reappeared from the direction of the sheer faces.

His cry was hawk-harsh and bitter with pain. "Thea! Ah, Thea! Why did you leave me—" Then he charged up the bluffs toward those fearsome unknown heights and was gone.

Later, as Oren returned along the road to Chelney, and despite the throb of his nose, he tried to think of what use he could make of his new knowledge.

"Luck is on my side," he told himself. "Siri and the girl cry out for each other, yet fate kept them apart today, and arranged that I could see it all."

Then suddenly it came to him that this knowledge might be a lever to obtain what he avidly desired. His pain seemed to fade a little now that he saw how he could be doubly revenged.

14

August passed, and toward the end of September the cold winds began. They promised an early winter this year. The rabbits, the muskrats, the otters, the beavers along the inland streams had fine heavy pelts. Only the resident birds remained. The season had been a good one for the fishing fleet. No one cared that it would end early. There had not been enough hands to do the heavy work and the men were exceedingly weary.

Beyond the bitter fatigue there was a miasma of fear that had hovered over the village for the past months. The only young people remaining to

Chelney besides the smaller children were a few girls on the edge of womanhood and trained to timidity, several slow-witted fellows, and Oren Sunderman. Some of the old people had also left, to live with son or daughter in places far from Chelney. Still, there remained the men and women in their middle life, able-bodied and vigorous. They saw no fault within themselves that would account for Chelney's decline, and so, with superstitious rumors and whisperings they sought the cause of the growing disaster.

Bartel Sunderman felt at the peak of his powers. The departure of so many young men did not disturb him. The young were restless, full of questions, and could be a danger to him. Besides, Oren had shown no desire to leave.

When several villagers came to Bartel to voice their fears over this loss of their young, Bartel said coldly, "It's your own fault. You've been too easy on them. When you have five, as I do, a man learns to rule with a heavy hand." He hitched his trousers a little, smiled. "Even my wife dances when I call the tune."

Still, there were enough men to do the work of the village, and now fewer mouths to feed. Besides, Sunderman had great plans for Chelney. First, he would order firmer measures to be taken with the children so when they came of an age to be of some use they would be more docile than those before them. When necessary, a belt, properly used, did much to break a wayward spirit.

As for Oren, his summer had been filled with growing frustration and anger. His nose had been slow to heal and remained ridiculously askew in his square face. There were few days he did not sail with the seiner that he coveted for his own. Aboard, he continued doggedly to watch his father for any sign of the deteriorations that come with age. It irritated him that the man remained robust and hearty. On the days when he was free, Oren haunted the flats south of town near the Duquesne cottage. These vigils fed the frustration.

Thea stayed closely sequestered. When she did appear it was always with the Old Woman. The girl was no longer so sleekly round, her gaze seldom lifted to another's. Her apparent fragility appealed to the waiting Oren. He remembered the ferocity of her defense and did not mind the thought that now she would be easier to subdue. Yet he could accomplish nothing in that direction as long as she was with the Old Woman.

Once he did catch her alone on the Chelney road between the village and the cottage. It was a Sunday and she had gone on, as she had that other time, while the Old Woman remained to chat outside the church. This day, though, Oren saw that the girl did not move with purpose. He found her easy to overtake. It was not until he roughly seized her arm near the shoulder that she was aware of his presence. Despite her withdrawn air, fear sprang up in her eyes again, giving a kind of life to the sharp features. This pleased Oren. He was further titillated when she tried to pull away. Oren tightened his grip, all the while watching warily for any sign of fight.

"Thea. That's your name," he said.

Her gaze flew to the road behind them. It was empty and he laughed. But he became doubly wary for now he saw that those intense eyes were not subdued despite her previously dejected air.

"Thea. That's the name Siri called up there on the hillside. Remember the day you broke my nose? I owe you something for that, Thea."

He did not know whether she flinched at the words or at the tightening of his meaty hand on her arm. The faint color along the high bones of her cheeks drained away.

"You saw him then?" She kept her voice steady and stared into his eyes, but despite her fear of Oren Sunderman her heart sang, *Ah, Siri, you have not forgotten me then.*

"Yes. He went past me out toward the base of the cliffs." His pale eyes squinted down at her. "I saw you come from there earlier. Some place you and Siri were used to meeting?"

"Let me go," she whispered and tried again to pull away.

Without releasing her, Oren said, "Siri will bring you nothing but trouble. It's only through Satan's help he's still alive." But it was plain that the girl's ears and mind were closed to anything he might say. She glanced back along the road again, and this time saw the Old Woman off in the distance.

Thea's voice was flat, but the fear was gone as she stared at him with acute distaste. "Emma will be here in a moment. Take your hand off me and be gone." She offered no threat but her tone had become ominous.

Oren, seeing they were no longer alone on the Chelney road, released her, and she moved to meet the woman, who was still some distance away. It was the sudden quietness of Oren's voice that stopped her.

"You had better listen, for Siri's sake," he said. "Did you know he is Chelney's outcast because he's an evil one? The people would gladly kill him if they could find him. A year and a half ago they would have burned him to death. That's the only sure way to deal with one of Satan's own. But he and his harpy disappeared together."

"You are surely mad," Thea breathed. "The bird you call a harpy was only a sea hawk. Siri told me of it. Yet he said nothing of the wickedness of the people of Chelney until the day I left him, and then only that you were all unnatural in your cruelty."

Oren glanced quickly in the direction of the Old Woman, who was drawing nearer. "I can tell my father about you and Siri. Everybody thinks Chelney is dying. They're scared out of their wits, and are beginning to turn against my father. It wouldn't be hard to convince them their trouble is still caused by Siri's evil, and then if my father could lead them to Siri, why—" And Oren shrugged and smiled and watched her through his pale lashes.

"You would not. Oh, surely—" Thea began. But she saw that pleading would only delight him and change his purpose not at all.

"Of course, if you were nice to me, I might forget that I saw Siri," Oren said.

She turned and ran toward the Old Woman. Already her mind desperately sought some way to help Siri. But she could not bear to think of bending to Oren Sunderman.

His voice followed her. "I wouldn't say anything if you warmed to me. Someday I'll be the biggest man in Chelney."

But Thea continued to run without looking back. Oren moved out into the countryside so he would not have to face the Old Woman in the narrow road. He circled back toward Chelney. Thea noted this and hope sprang up. The way was open to the cliffs and the cave.

"What did that lout want?" asked Emma as the girl turned to walk beside her toward the cottage. Thea smiled faintly and the woman saw that at least the girl's cheeks held a little color now.

"He was trying to tell me what an important fellow he will be someday in Chelney," Thea said.

The Old Woman snorted and said nothing more. And Thea wondered how she would pass the hours until late afternoon. It was then she would be most likely to find Siri if he had truly returned to the cave.

Bartel Sunderman sat in his own house, his feet propped on the hearthstone. A small fire burned there, for the chilly wind had sprung up again in the early afternoon. He waited for his wife to bring him a cup of strong tea and the one pipe of tobacco he allowed himself of a Sunday. He ordered his children about, sending them on this errand or that to gratify his sense of command even in his own house. Oren came in and settled too. The man frowned. He couldn't quite put his finger on it, but Oren had begun to irritate him of late with his long speculative looks.

For a change though, today, Oren said something that caught his interest.

"We thought Siri was gone from Chelney or that he was dead," Oren began. Bartel raised his brows in surprise and grunted around his pipe as his son continued. "He's alive as I am and he hasn't gone away either." Oren reared back in the chair, asserting his own importance now.

"And how do you know that?" Bartel asked.

"Through the girl. Her name's Thea. Thea Duquesne, the Old Woman says."

"Thea Duquesne talks with you?"

"When I force her to." Oren laughed. "You were right that girls pretend to be frightened or that they don't even see you to give an air of modesty. But I know how she truly feels. It is fun, though, when they pull away and tremble so."

"Even your mother once did." Bartel chuckled, pleased that he still had her a little cowed after all the years. But then he turned serious. "Where does that Devil's changeling keep himself then?"

"I can't tell you yet." Oren's look evaded his father's. "I think the girl will lead me to him, though."

"She knows Siri?"

Oren winked at the man. "I'm sure of it."

"And she will lead us to Siri?"

"Lead *me* to Siri," Oren corrected. "You and I will have to keep this whole thing secret. If everyone knows, they'll go out there whooping and shouting, and our chicken will fly the roost. We'll have to be smart about it. Once before I followed Thea and she lost me, but this time I'll stick close as a tick." He watched the man turn this in his mind. "When I know where Siri hides, I'll come back and tell you." Then Oren began to grin. "When we finally bring him in, I'm sure Thea Duquesne will come my way."

Bartel gave his son a long look before nodding with satisfaction. "Last year a boy, today a man, lusty as his father." Then, half to himself, "And clever."

But beneath the satisfaction lay distrust. *The young challenge the old*, he reminded himself, *and a man seeks to displace a man.* And suddenly he understood the brooding watchfulness he had seen in his son's face. He determined to keep a wary eye on all that transpired.

She waited until the hill lay in shadow, though the flats were still streaked with the September sun. The Old Woman was asleep in her chair and the Old Man continued to stare unseeing at the rafters. Thea slipped outside. She scanned the road for any villager who might have taken the unfrequented way for a late stroll. It was empty.

She flew down its lonely length and out into the open countryside. Her whole mind was on Siri and how she could persuade him of his danger. There were other places than Chelney; they could go away together. The uneasy thought came, perhaps he wouldn't believe her, perhaps he had turned cold toward her. Presently she reached the beginning of the hillside. It was as she entered the woods that Oren stepped into the open. He fully blocked her way. She knew herself to be more nimble than he, but with time he could run her to ground. He stood there smiling at her, sure of himself.

"Don't tell me that you've decided to give in to me to keep Siri safe! Still, what other reason for you to come and meet me so willingly?"

There was sarcasm in his words. He moved toward her, glad he had made this bold move despite what he had told Bartel of cunning and stealth. He reached for the girl's arm. "I was sure what I told you earlier would drive you from the Old Woman's protection. You think you'll warn Siri against me." Again he lunged toward her. "Now do not fight so fiercely this time. I can make you suffer for it." He continued to smile, but watched her warily as he maneuvered to trap her.

Thea avoided his hand, fell back a step or two. "Let me past," she said. "Then I might come to you later. And more pleasantly, too." She tried to smile, and she kept her voice persuasive.

When he laughed and said, "You think I would trust you for that?" she turned and ran back along the way to Chelney. At first she outdistanced him. Yet the Old Woman's cottage was too far away and slowly he gained. Suddenly angling to the right he cut her off from the cottage and even the village beyond. She whirled about to make one try for the hill where her agility and stamina would count. Despite his bulk, he was quicker than she had thought. As skillfully as though seining for fish, he passed between her and the hill. He aimed to keep her on the flats, to force her into the thickets near the swamp. There they would be hidden and undisturbed. He gave a grunt of triumph as, in desperation, she turned and fled toward the swamp's edge. It surprised him when she crashed through the fringe and continued into the musty quaking land beyond.

"Better take your chances with me than a sinkhole!" he shouted gleefully. He forgot his fear of the marshy place. The girl would be the one to find the first quagmire, and he would still be safe. It was even easy to imagine himself pulling her free. She would be subdued and grateful, and he would not mind the mud.

As for Thea, she had no fear of anything but Oren Sunderman. She had explored these ways with Siri and he had shown her the safe paths. Now she skirted one treacherous spot, leaped another, and did not penetrate deeply into unknown places. Here her nimbleness served well. Slowly she began to outdistance Oren. For one moment, now, she dodged from his sight, skirted a wide sinkhole on a narrow footway, sprang over the last bit, grabbed a sturdy bush, swung out of sight.

Oren was into the sucking ooze before he knew it was there. His bullish strength allowed him to struggle toward its center, certain that the girl had managed it safely. With horror, Thea watched as he was mired. She had only sought to hide while he passed her by. With dreadful slowness he began to sink. She had not consciously intended this. Frantically she scrambled about looking for some branch or downed sapling that would bridge the pit and allow him to pull his great bulk free. She was certain he had lost that ardent interest in the chase.

In a frenzy, Oren grunted and struggled. He loosened one foot by thrusting the other more deeply. Then he changed the effort in order to free the second. He lost his balance, sank deeper. Thus mired, he settled halfway between hip and knee.

Terrified, his eyes huge and white-rimmed, he screamed to Thea, "Throw me that branch there!"

"It's too short." Nevertheless she threw it to quiet him. He snatched it from the air, probed the sucking mud to no avail, tried to reach the solid shore with it, could not, flung it away. The stubby wood lay useless for a moment then quietly sank from sight. The slight crease left in the chocolate ooze gradually flattened. A slow bubble of air broke the surface. It was this last that threw Oren into further frenzy.

"Find something!" he squealed. "Oh God! Help me! Help me! I'm sinking! I'll die! It's that Siri! He called up the Devil's curse on me. Oh God, God—" And he continued to struggle, which quickly settled him in the quagmire to his hips.

Thea rushed here and there trying for some sturdier support to help him. With an effort she kept her voice calm. "Stand quietly. Do not flail about. You will sink more slowly if you don't struggle."

216

"Damn you! Go get help! Before it's too late!" Oren bellowed.

She hesitated one moment, then leaped away through the brushy fringe into the open flats. She could hear his screams, witless with terror. "Don't leave me! Oh, hurry. Oh, God help me! Oh, the Devil, the Devil—"

It was only luck that sent the Old Woman back toward the village to look for Thea. The girl was gone from the cottage when she herself had awakened from a short Sabbath nap. Now it was getting late. She had two worries. The first, that Thea had left her again to search for Siri; the other, her memory of Oren and the way he had looked at the girl. As she neared the edge of the village she saw Bartel Sunderman coming her way.

"Think of Satan's imp, and Satan himself appears," she muttered, and wondered what business the man had in this direction at twilight on a Sunday. She tried to pass him with no word, but he spoke to her.

"Have you seen my Oren?" he asked.

"I've seen no one," she answered and would not say she looked for Thea. It worried her, though, that those two were missing at the same time. The sun had set, a lavender haze hung over the flats, the air had chilled. The man and woman were about to pass each other by when a voice called out from the direction of the marshes. It was with relief that Emma saw the girl running toward them. Yet a strange foreboding seized her as she waited.

For a breath or two, Thea was incoherent. When she finally cried out the name, Oren, Emma thought her own fears were confirmed. She grabbed Thea's shoulder, shook her.

"Stop that trembling and crying," she said sternly. "Now what of Oren? Has he done aught to harm you?"

"He's caught in the bog," Thea managed to gasp, then to Bartel, "Quick, oh, quickly! You'll need a long timber, or a ladder, or rope, or—" She controlled the hysteria that climbed in her throat.

"The blasted young fool," Bartel grated. But even as he spoke, he turned and ran toward the nearest house. In seconds he spotted a coil of rope cast down at one end of a porch. He lunged for it as a man came to the door of the house.

Before the man could speak, Bartel shouted at him, "My boy is caught in a sinkhole! Get some of the men and come as fast as you can. Bring a ship's spar to bridge the hole. Hurry! Hurry!"

The man dashed off. Bartel grabbed up the rope, turned on Thea. At the terrible look in the man's eyes, Thea whirled, and like a deer startled from cover, fled toward the swamp. Bartel could scarcely keep pace. For some reason the Old Woman followed, moving as rapidly as she could, though she was immediately left behind.

Thea listened for the sound of Oren Sunderman's voice. The late air was heavy with silence. In her panic had she failed to note the place properly? No. No. She was certain. The creek off to the left, the old oak there. Yet, now the deadly silence.

"Hurry, you little witch!" grated Bartel as he caught up with her. "Oren told me about you and Siri. We thought the Duquesne boy dead. Did you cast a spell on Oren to lead him here? Chelney knows how to deal with Satan's brood—"

But Thea closed her mind to the ugly voice and pushed through the tangle of vines and brush. Bartel crashed along at her heels. When she paused for an instant to get her bearing, the quiet was more fearsome than Bartel's threats. Then, sure of the place, Thea dashed forward. Yes, there through the gloom, the quagmire she had skirted earlier. Under the thick canopy of rank growth, twilight had become evening. In the center of the bog she saw Oren, his face a pallid misshapen moon, his hands extended upward. He had sunk to his armpits. Drugged with his own terror at the imminent, awful death, he had ceased to struggle. Now he was unaware that help had come. His lips moved but no sound came forth.

"Oren." Bartel's voice choked. It was a fearful sight, for his son continued to settle slowly, slowly. "I'll throw the rope to you. Grab it, try to pass it around your chest beneath your arms."

But Oren did not respond. His eyes stared, unseeing, past the man and the girl. He seemed beyond any help. Bartel hesitated, moved to the edge of the bog as though to plunge in and save his witless son. Was it fear that stopped the man at the brink, or his instinctive knowledge that Oren had become impatient for his death in order to usurp his place as captain of the seiner and Leader of Chelney? Whatever the reason, Bartel stood unmoving, horrified but unable to sacrifice himself.

Cold with terror, Thea tied one end of the rope about her own waist, gauged the distance, then fastened the center of the line around a sturdy bush. Silently, Bartel watched her. She took the free end of the rope in her hands and edged along the brink to the spot nearest Oren. It was only her slight weight and wiry strength that allowed her to force her way to his side. He was a great unresponsive slug sinking in the slime, but she managed to pass the rope around him beneath his arms, tie it securely across his chest. The sucking mud had snatched her down above her knees by the time she was finished.

Bartel, who had made no move to help her, now began to take in the slack of the end that secured his son. Thea no longer cared about them. It took all of her strength to haul herself from the quagmire with the aid of the length she had twisted about the bush. Silently she untied the rope from her waist. Oblivious of the stinking mud that caked her lower body, she pushed out of the close fetid place into the fresh evening air of the open flats. Several men rushed past lugging a heavy spar. Preoccupied with their urgent mission they scarcely seemed to see her. Thea did not turn her head to watch them. She was through with the people of Chelney. Instead she moved out across the dry grass, and after a bit blundered, unseeing, into the Old Woman.

"Did you find Oren?" asked Emma Duquesne.

"Yes." Thea's voice scarcely broke the silence. A thin chill breeze that whispered of winter crept across the flats.

"Will they be able to get him out?"

"I think so."

"Ah." It was difficult to tell whether Emma was relieved or sorry.

With a great effort, Thea roused her own numb mind. She embraced the woman despite the stiff resistance of the old body. "Now truly I must leave you. Good-bye, dear Emma."

"No. You will be safe here with me." Emma ignored the farewell.

"I would not be safe. Even with you. Oren told his father of Siri and where he could be found. Now Bartel Sunderman says we both are evil and bound to Satan. He threatened that Chelney knows how to deal with evil ones."

"*Ah-h-h.*" The Old Woman's breath hissed in scorn and when she spoke her voice was bitter as gall. "Bartel is our evil. He would destroy Siri and you and all of Chelney!" After a moment Emma Duquesne continued, "Yes, you must go. Perhaps you can persuade Siri to leave with you. Though I doubt it." She gave a short harsh laugh. But the next instant she groaned. "I had him for a few years, then he became a stranger. Now I lose you too and am left with only sorrow and bitterness."

Thea embraced her again. This time the Old Woman's body was limp with defeat and the two clung together.

"Only remember, I love you, and shall even when I'm gone," the girl whispered. "Think of me with love and your sorrow will ease, the bitterness will die."

Then Thea pulled away and was gone, fleeing toward the south where the cliffs rose black against the night sky.

PART FIVE

The Sanctuary

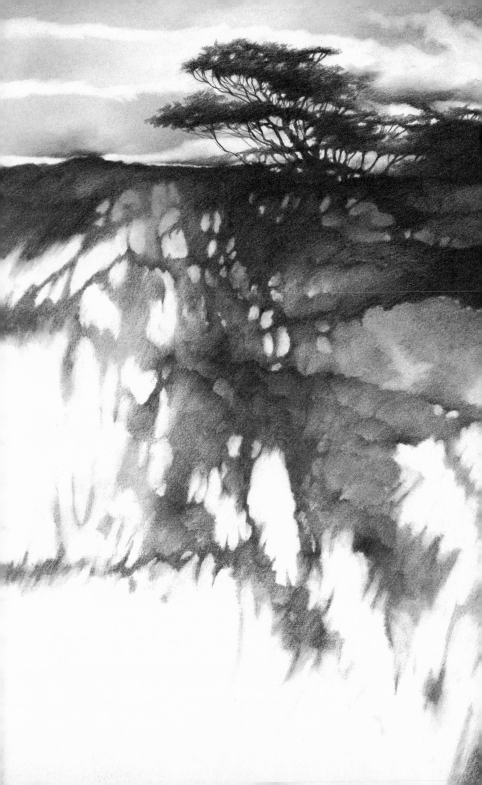

15

Tonight the October wind was as chill and solitary as his own soul. Siri knew it was beyond the power of his body or mind to change further. He could never join the ospreys who had flown south at the end of summer. That last day, even the old hawk regarded him with detachment and did not hesitate to forsake him when he was unable to join the final flight. But then, Siri had no real desire to leave Chelney's coast.

Now, he stood alone on the rim of the night sky. The cliffs fell away below him to the edge of the sea. Along the thick silken growth that covered his body and limbs he felt the hand of winter. This disturbed him not at all. Nor did it sadden him in any way to know that he was forever separate from all men, and also unable to fully join the creatures of the wild. On this evening, with no line to mark dream from reality, it seemed he stretched great pinions, launched himself outward, exulted in the short free turn in the black air, swooped up, came to rest on the cliff's rim once more. Then, equally impervious to sorrow or regret or cold or the windy dark, he settled, bent his head, curled in upon himself and slept.

It was with a terrible reluctance, a piercing anguish that he came awake. He had forgotten the girl long ago. He had even forgotten the agony of that forgetting. Yet on this night she had returned to haunt his dreams. He tried to snatch at sleep again. He curled more tightly, enfolding his head with his arms, hooding himself with the projections along back and shoulders. Yet, persistently, even though he had come fully awake, her voice called and called. When at last he could deny the fact of her presence no longer, he sprang to his feet. No dream this apparition. Thea had returned. Coldly he watched as she ran across the barren ground.

The light of the stars and the quarter moon were dimmed by streamers of cloud that strung themselves across the high dark. Used to lamp-light and village ways, Thea did not see the figure looming there, motionless, in the night.

She continued toward the south where the plateau lifted to the higher cliffs of the headland. Siri let her go and did not try to follow. Yet presently she rushed back, frightened by the strange wild place and the rising wind that blew colder than before. Where earlier she had called his name, now he heard only the low sob of her breath. He would have let her pass again, so she could return to the lowlands and the Old Woman and the village for which she had longed and left him, but she sank down, overwhelmed with the terrors of the day and the fear of what was yet to come.

Siri drew a little nearer as she began openly and hopelessly to cry. He remained silent. At last, completely spent, she neither cried nor moved. It was then his own old pain sprang to full life once more. He grew angry, for he had thought himself done with all of that. At last he could stand it no longer and drew near, bent, touched her. The round little head came up, and he could see the wide frightened eyes and the sharp face and the prominent teeth, and beneath his hand she moved and the sleek roundness was still there though she was much thinner than he remembered.

"Thea," he whispered, afraid of his own voice

that had grown harsh as a hawk's.

She sprang up, flung herself toward him.

"Ah, Siri, Siri, Siri," she cried out softly, but he withdrew from her, sure that the changes in him would terrify her.

"Don't be angry with me still," she pleaded. "I tried to find you. But you were gone, gone. Why didn't you come for me?" She peered at him in the dim light. "Siri?"

He refused to withdraw further, but stood boldly, not hiding himself. "I looked for you in the cave. But I thought you had forgotten me."

"Oh, no—" she whispered, "never—"

His voice was distant, cool. "Now I've changed and you will find me ugly and frightening. Go back to Chelney. Leave while it is dark and remember me that other way."

For a moment the clouds cleared the moon, and in the stronger light she could see him there. Then came the quick memory of her meager early years; and the short hope that the sailor had given her; and then the *Laura Ann*. She remembered the bowels of the ship and the avid careless crew. She remembered Oren Sunderman, and the recent terror of him in the marshy thickets. Even the Old Woman loved through sorry need. Only with this strange boy had love passed freely between her and another.

231

This time when she came softly to him, Siri did not retreat. Her arms came around him. He felt her hands on the sharp angles of his face, the jut of his nose, the stiff crown that sprang above his forehead, then along his shoulders and arms and the strangeness of his back, down the planes of his silken body and hips and thighs. She came against him as he remembered. And she whispered to him over and again, "I love you, Siri—" She was within his arms. They stood thus, unspeaking, until the eternity apart dissolved and was forgotten. Then they lay down upon the hard stone together and found comfort in each other. The night wind did not penetrate their love.

When the clouds thickened and a light rain began to fall, he led her to a slanted outcrop of rock. They were able to edge beneath this and lie there, unaware of the rain, unfeeling of the cold. Together they were warm. Later, toward morning, she told him of Chelney and the Old Man and Old Woman. And also of Oren and Bartel Sunderman. He held her more closely and she was consoled. She told him, too, why they must leave and find a life elsewhere.

"I cannot," Siri finally answered. "In any town the people would scorn me. There would be no way we could live. And wild, where could I survive except here along Chelney's coast?"

For this Thea had no answer. He still continued to hold her as he promised himself aloud. "I'll not be driven away."

"Then I shall stay here with you." And now, contented, Thea lay quietly in his arms. After a while, though, she asked, "What will we do if they come and try to take us?"

Siri laughed, the old bold fearless laugh. "They're afraid of this high place. They think it cursed. That will keep us safe." But in his mind was the memory of the fire the villagers had planned for the female osprey and finally would have used to destroy him too.

And now there was Thea.

Quietly he said, "They will never take us back to Chelney."

Bartel Sunderman stood staring at his son. The man burned with humiliation and despair. A week had passed since they had saved Oren from the bog. That night was seared in Bartel's memory when with the help of the other men, he had pried the bulky body from the muddy suck. The body, yes, but not the mind. That had stayed somewhere in the dark swamp. Now Oren could only mumble and stare at something no one else saw. Bartel was certain that the men and women of Chelney snickered behind his back. The final blow to the man's pride came when, in passing through the village on this very day, he saw the small children harrying his son as once they had been led to torment Siri Duquesne.

"But for the girl, Oren would be dead," the man muttered. He did not admit, even to himself, that he would have preferred it so rather than suffer such shame over his witless son. "Still, if she had come for help more quickly that day of the swamp, he would not have been driven out of his mind with terror."

As he mulled this over, his despair slowly turned to rage. "Siri and the girl planned it that way. Between them, Oren was tormented past all endurance. Who can guess what they did to him? And the Old Woman was in on it, too. It is she who has been hinting that Oren followed the girl into the bushes with some thought of taking her. As any lusty fellow might! Is that such a crime?" His outrage grew. "Satan's trio," he whispered darkly. "The Old Woman. The girl. Siri. The Devil uses them to destroy us all. But they will see, they will see."

Sunderman's eyes gleamed and part of his lost pride was restored as he made his plans. Oren's plight no longer weighed upon him; it was a mother's duty to see to blighted young ones.

That night Bartel Sunderman called the men to

the Meeting House. He insisted they all be present despite the worsening weather. The women were ordered to stay at home. Women were always argumentative and full of dissension. At first the men refused to fall in with Bartel's plan, for he told them they must start this very evening. When he saw he might fail entirely, he compromised.

"Darkness is our ally. But if you're afraid of the night, then the early morning hours will have to serve our purpose," he said largely. "We'll start well before dawn tomorrow." But he himself was relieved at this decision, for now they would have the light of day for their descent and triumphant return to the village, captives in hand.

"The clouds and wind will further hide our movements," he assured the men. "We'll fall upon those two before they know we're there."

"Do you plan to kill them on the spot?" one of the group asked as they all glanced uneasily at one another. Bartel's face, which had once seemed merely stupid, now looked malignant to them.

"No," he said. "We want them alive. *Alive.* Tomorrow night a great fire outside the Meeting House will end all our difficulties," he laughed. "And theirs also. You will see."

The men remained silent, looking at the ground. They no longer trusted Sunderman as

Leader, but each was afraid to say so. They wondered what dark corners of their own souls had made them follow him before. And still.

Through the black end of night before morning, the hunters moved warily across the flats, up the lower slopes to the juncture of hillside and cliff. They had lost part of their guilty fear and now began to grumble over this fool's chase Sunderman had arranged.

But Sunderman said, "We begin our search here. Oren told me that those two have some meeting place not far from this spot."

So, reluctantly, they began a confused hunt for any sign of Siri and the girl. The wind buffeted them and rain fell intermittantly, with occasional spits of snow to warn of worse to come. The hooded lanterns they carried made small patches of light that moved erratically about the slopes. Presently one of the men blundered into the cave. In a moment he had called the others and they gathered there out of the cold. Now a little excitement began to rise and their anger at Sunderman faded. They made a thorough inspection of the cave. They found the strange nest and the oddments the Old Woman had brought and other dusty evidence that the boy and girl had once lived here. The men were amazed that Siri had managed to survive last winter's cold. Now, though, the cave showed long disuse.

For some reason, the discovery of the cave lifted their spirits. When they did not find the boy there, spurred on by Sunderman's resolve, they began the steeper ascent toward the top of the bluffs. The rain gave way almost entirely to the wet sleety snow. This fell thinly and was snatched away by the vicious wind. Near the top the clouds closed around them, scudded past, spilled over the edge to snag on cliffy shelves below.

At first they had hoped the climb would be too difficult, for all of them were still terribly afraid of these mysterious heights. Then they would be forced to return home. Yet so strange is the lust of man turned hunter that when they succeeded in gaining the top and stood there on the stormy plateau, they were exhilarated and saw themselves as bold and mighty. Forgetting their fear, they inspected their guns, checked triggers, bolts, released safeties, assured themselves that all was in readiness.

Sunderman, still avid to take the pair alive, warned the men to use the guns only as a last resort. Yet he carried his own at the ready. Despite the clouds, the eastern sky began to brighten as they started across the plateau. The snow proved a blessing. The scant fall had gathered in small depressions, and thus defined a number of shallow footprints in the gritty soil. They concentrated their effort in the area where the prints appeared more thickly. Sunderman handled his gun with hands tense and restless on stock and trigger. He feared that somehow Siri would escape him, and the girl also. He was finished in Chelney if he failed here.

The men bent to closely inspect the ground before them. It was only Sunderman who scanned the whole area as it gradually brightened in the murky dawn. Wind-driven snakes of cloud coiled across the plateau. At first he thought the movement was one of these. He leaned forward, squinted. *No.* Shadow moved on shadow. Two ghostly figures. The rough semicircle of men closed in toward the cliff's edge as they discovered prints here and there. Sunderman saw that the two obscured figures were trapped in this half-noose of hunters.

"You, Siri!" The man's voice cut through wind and storm. "Stop where you are!" And he raised his gun. The blast stunned the men. They looked wildly about and saw nothing. Sunderman had not meant to fire so quickly. He still wanted them both alive. He continued to shout. He was certain the smaller of the ghostly shadows faltered. The larger scooped this one close, then both melted swiftly toward the cliff's rim.

"Close in!" Sunderman cried. "We have them trapped against the edge!"

There were shouts from one and then another, triumphant, avid for the quarry. The men rushed forward.

"I see them! There! There!" echoed all up and down the line. But the wind fell away, the clouds closed in, and all was obscured for a breath of time.

Though, later, each claimed he had seen Thea and Siri Duquesne on that storm-whipped rim, only two of the men swore they saw the fugitives leap into space. And finally one of these two became uncertain and said he was not sure if it was truly the pair they had been seeking.

"Perhaps a great bird," he mumbled. "It whirled down and down as though it fell. You must remember there were clouds. It was difficult to see—"

But all of that was said later. The truth was that on the day of the high hunt they had seen something moving through the mist, yet when they reached the cliff's rim, there was nothing. They found only one sign that Sunderman had not missed his shot—a small pool of blood and beside it, the partial print of a slender foot.

"The girl. It was she I hit. The little witch," Sunderman insisted. "And Siri picked her up. See, here is a strange print, not hers, and another there in that other pocket of snow near the cliff's edge."

"And yet it is not a boy's print either," one of the men said, but the rest ignored him.

"They are dead on the rocks below," Sunderman declared. "There is no way at all they could have escaped. I tell you, we will find them below."

It was almost noon before they managed to descend the bluffs, slick with snow, and make their way to the rocky beach above the waves. The tide had been low during the early part of the day. Now it was beginning to rise. They were certain it would not be difficult to find the bodies of Siri and the girl. Yet some of the men wanted to return to the village. They remembered sons of their own, lost to them when the boys departed Chelney. And daughters gone away who would never return. Now the men thought of Emma Duquesne. If they found Siri dead, how would they explain this to her? And the Old Woman had taken the girl in like one of her own.

Sunderman was adamant. They searched through the afternoon. No body was found. At last, one by one, the men drifted away. Each, separately, returned to his own home. By nightfall

240

Sunderman was alone. Finally darkness and the tide drove him from the beach. He stood for a long time on the slope below the cliffs, staring down at the lights of Chelney. The men had left him alone and he knew that all the villagers were finished with him. Nothing remained for him in Chelney.

Unless—

Slowly, then, he smiled, and began the climb up the bluffs. He had remembered that day, so long ago, when they had captured the female osprey. It was Siri who had insisted then that too many hunters would blight the hunt. And so it had proved earlier on this day when the pair had escaped the noisy, bumbling men.

The sky had cleared, the wind had lessened. The man continued upward in the cold silence, comforted by the gun in his hand. Tonight, alone, he would avenge his son, delight his own dark soul, and prove himself truly the Leader of Chelney.

Next morning, out of pity for Bartel's wife, a few of the men returned to the beach below the cliffs. Briefly they wondered if the early low tide would reveal Siri and the girl dead there on the harsh shore. Ice had formed during the night in the shadows beneath the rocks. The small life at the water's edge was sluggish or absent. Some of the resident birds were busy on their morning search for food. The shadow of wings slid across the men from time to time.

It was midmorning when they found Bartel Sunderman. Apparently he had fallen from some great height above. They turned their faces from the grisly sight and covered what was left of him with stones. They knew that in time the scuttling crabs and the sea would cleanse the shore. Then the men returned to Chelney.

A few families, taking all the goods they could crowd on board their modest boats, left the village that same day. And several more the next. And so it continued until winter set in.

When spring came only the Old Woman was left. The Old Man had not survived February's arctic cold. It was April before the ice was gone, and May when the supply boat came with its first delivery of the season. The men aboard the *Sea Horse* could scarcely believe that of all the village of Chelney, only Emma Duquesne remained. She seemed none the worse for the solitary life, appearing vigorous and clear of eye. She said she had no intention of leaving. In a way they could not blame her. The coast was beautiful with the burgeoning spring. There were birds in great profusion this year, the willows and grasses were tender green, the streams and the waters of the estuaries were lucent, pure, glittering in the clear spring light. The old orchard was adrift with blossoms, promising a fine crop next fall. Emma Duquesne's place was in good repair, though already the houses of the village had the air of long neglect. It seemed impossible to the men that she could manage so well alone. Yet the evidence was before them. There was certainly no one left to help her.

They delivered enough supplies to keep the Old Woman, and promised to stop on their next trip north. In the morning before they sailed, one of the men made his way out to the set-apart cottage. He found the Old Woman in the yard, gazing toward the cliffy land to the south.

"Do you remember me?" he asked. "I taught here in the Chelney school for a couple of seasons. But that was years ago."

Emma Duquesne looked him over with her cool gaze.

"Yes," she said. "I remember you." And let the conversation die.

The man tried again. "I came along on the *Sea Horse* this trip to see if the coast had changed since I was here."

Emma studied him for a long silent moment. Finally she asked, "And has it?"

He smiled then, thinking he had engaged her.

"Well, of course the village is different with the people gone. The land is wilder. And there are more birds than I remember. A number of ospreys were over the northern tideflats as we came into harbor. My work at the university has to do with birds. We thought the ospreys were gone from the entire coast here."

She nodded. "With the village empty, things go well for the wild ones."

Presently, though, he said, "There was a boy when I taught in Chelney's school. He's stayed in my mind all this time. He was the only one eager and able to learn. His name was Siri. Always full of questions about the wild things here. We used to have long talks." The man smiled. "We learned from each other." Then he shook his head, half sadly. "The boy was unlike the other solemn children."

The Old Woman glanced at him, then bent to pull a weed from beside the path.

The man persisted. "Is Siri gone with all the others?"

The woman gave a quick little laugh, swept her hand toward the empty village and at the vacant road. "As you can see, he's not about."

A shadow of wings swept across the sun. The man turned and gazed toward the south, but the birds disappeared in the dazzle of spring light.

"Ospreys?" he asked, puzzled.

"Most of the sea hawks nest in the snags along the north estuary. There may be some, though, on the cliffs south of here."

But before the man could ask anything further, the Old Woman turned away to her own business and left him standing there alone.

Format by Kohar Alexanian
Set in 12 pt. Janson
Composed and bound by The Haddon Craftsmen,
Scranton, Penna.
Printed by The Murray Printing Company
HARPER & ROW, PUBLISHERS, INC.

359

F
JON

Jones, Adrienne
The hawks of Chelney

DATE			
MR 17 '82			
NO 8 '82			